A Horse for
ELSIE

A Horse for
ELSIE

AN AMISH CHRISTMAS ROMANCE

LINDA BYLER

Good Books®

New York, New York

A HORSE FOR ELSIE

Good Books books may be purchased in bulk at special discounts for sales promotion, corporate gifts, fund-raising, or educational purposes. Special editions can also be created to specifications. For details, contact the Special Sales Department, Good Books, 307 West 36th Street, 11th Floor, New York, NY 10018 or info@skyhorsepublishing.com.

Good Books is an imprint of Skyhorse Publishing, Inc.®, a Delaware corporation.

Visit our website at www.goodbooks.com.

10 9 8 7 6 5 4 3 2 1

Library of Congress Cataloging-in-Publication Data is available on file.

ISBN: 978-1-68099-383-7
eBook ISBN: 978-1-68099-384-4

Cover design by Jenny Zemanek

Printed in the United States of America

Table of Contents

Chapter One

ELSIE STOOD AT THE METAL YARD GATE beneath the old white oak tree, one foot tucked up under her purple skirt, the other planted solidly on the fractured cement sidewalk, and glared at the pony and cart trotting gaily past their driveway. The pony was perfect—small, round, and compact, the way all Shetland ponies are. But this pony was special in the way he arched his thick, short neck and raised his hooves high, looking as regal as could be.

He was driven by Elam Stoltzfus, a boy from seventh grade, one grade above her own. Elam was bold, as proud as his pony. She had asked him once if she could drive the pony, but he had told her airily that anyone who had no experience with ponies could not drive this one. He'd give her a ride sometime, but no, she could not drive.

His little brother, Benny, sat beside him today, his straw hat smashed down so far Elsie could only see a nose and a chin. What was the point of going for a ride if your eyes were stuck behind a straw hat? Boys were strange creatures with idiotic ideas—especially Benny. He claimed there were turtles as big as a cow that lived to be a hundred years old. Then, as if that wasn't hard enough to believe, he said they lived on an island she couldn't hope to pronounce and couldn't think of spelling, so she had tried to look it up in the *World Book Encyclopedia* but never found it. He was making it up, she was sure. She wasn't about to ask him how to spell the name of the island, either.

And there he went, sitting beside Elam driving that perfect pony. Elam was older than Benny but just as much of a know-it-all, especially when it came to horses. Elsie had read *Black Beauty* and all the Marguerite Henry books in the school library, so she knew a lot more about horses than those two thought she did.

The thing was, her family was poor. They could hardly afford hay and grain for their one stodgy old driving horse, let alone feed a pony or any sort of horse just for pleasure. So, Elsie never dared talk about wanting a horse of her own. When Elam talked about all their horses, she hung around to hear what he had to say, correcting him on occasion, but mostly thought he was too proud, even arrogant, boasting about that barn full of beautiful horses.

Elsie was the oldest in a family of five children, all girls—except Amos, who was only a year old and the biggest pest anyone could imagine. He was always underfoot, his nose ran constantly, he fell and hurt himself at least a dozen times a day. And who was yelled at to go rescue him? She was.

They all lived in an old farmhouse that wasn't their own place, the way other Amish people bought their homes. Elsie's father had been in a car accident on the way to work at the pallet shop in Kinzers and lost most of his right arm. Ever since then, he'd struggled to find work he could do that paid well enough to support the family. He was cheerful and thankful, appreciated the cheap rent, and loved the old farmhouse and the dilapidated barn that housed his old horse and rattling secondhand buggy. He loved every one of his children and said he was grateful for each day here on earth. He could have been killed that day, and then what?

Which was true.

Elsie couldn't imagine life without her happy father. He was everyone's sunshine, the spark that ignited all the good times. And there were plenty of good times. But being poor was a constant disappointment. When the other girls had new dresses and black aprons, brand-new name-brand sneakers and baseball gloves, Elsie knew she looked dowdy with her sneakers from the consignment shop on Strasburg Road, dresses that were her cousin's hand-me-downs, and a baseball glove that was too small and weathered to a dull brown, the laces loose and broken. When lunch boxes opened at dinner hour in school, she eyed the fancy granola bars in their shining wrappers, the bought containers of yogurt and Jello and pudding, the individual bags of Cheetos and potato chips, and did her best to hide her white American cheese sandwich in both hands. The bread was always homemade and crumbly, leaving telltale crumbs all over her lap and on her desktop. She had become an expert at swiping them onto the floor before the other children took notice.

Her mother made a fresh popper of popcorn almost every morning, unless she bought a huge bag of stick pretzels at Creekside Foods. She only did that when they were on sale. Popcorn worked really well, though, especially if it was seasoned with sour cream and onion powder. Rosanne Esh, in eighth grade, loved Elsie's popcorn and traded all sorts of delicious things to get her hands on it. Once, she handed over a ziplock bag containing chips that were stacked together, perfectly uniform and shaped like little cups. Too proud to ask what they were, Elsie merely reached into the bag and ate them one by one. It was the most delicious snack she had ever eaten. It was a big mystery, how anyone could make potato chips that weren't greasy or salty and that fit together so precisely.

Elsie was always impressed that the other girls had fancy new lunch boxes every year. Actually, some of them were like little purses with their names written on the front in fancy lettering. They said their mother bought them at a 31 Party. Whatever in the world that was, Elsie thought.

At recess, Elsie forgot about being poor. She was an avid baseball player, naturally athletic, with long, thin legs that propelled her around the ball diamond faster than the boys. She scooped up hard-drive grounders, caught flies, and threw the ball with amazing precision to yelling, hopping outfielders. It was a known fact that Elsie was always chosen long before some of the upper-grade boys, which usually sparked a few martyred sniffs from Elam. Oh, she knew what he was thinking. Girls should never be chosen to be on a team before guys, no matter how good they were.

Elsie always flashed him a triumphant look, before bouncing over to the team that had chosen her. *You drive your fancy pony, Elam. I get chosen before you, so there.*

Elsie guessed if she had not been born to an Amish family, she would be a player on some important team, wearing a uniform and a ball cap pulled low on her forehead, her hair in a ponytail. Wouldn't that be exciting? But she was Amish, and she loved her world, her people. She was fine with flying around the ball diamond in her faded green dress, the pins that held her black apron around her waist mostly intact, her hair in the bun on the back of her head loosening steadily as recess wore on. Mostly, she was content.

Except for this chafing ambition to own a pony, a harness, and a cart. Not just an ordinary pony, but one that ran down the road the way Elam Stoltzfus's pony did. Like a show horse. It gave her chills.

Someday, somehow, she would have a Shetland pony that ran as beautifully as Elam's pony, Cookie. Now what kind of name was that for a pony? A cat should be named Cookie. A pig or a parakeet, maybe. Not a pony. If she had a pony, she would name him something more inspired, like Lightning or Whiz or Dreamcatcher (Dream for short).

She turned when she heard a high-pitched sound coming from the sandbox beside the house. There was little Amos, his face lifted to the sky, screeching like a hyena, his eyes closed tightly, his mouth an open hole that emitted desperate sounds of agony. *Now what?*

Elsie turned and ran, flung herself on her knees, and reached for him, streaming nose and all. She found his hand stuck firmly inside the small opening of the metal watering can.

"Here, hold still. Stop yelling. Shh. Hush."

Nothing helped, so she tugged, twisted the child's

toy first one way, then another, until she freed the trapped, reddened little hand.

His yells increased with her efforts until they escalated to short, horrible shrieks of panic.

"Hush, Amos. It's all right."

Her mother's worried face appeared at a window, a moment before she dashed through the screen door, letting it close with that familiar slapping sound. She bounded down the steps and to the sandbox, holding out her arms, already crooning her baby nonsense that made Elsie's toes curl.

"*Komm, komm.* Poor little chap."

She lifted the corner of her gray apron to wipe his face, leaning back to blow his nose as he turned his head.

"I don't know why you do that. Use a handkerchief," Elsie said drily, swallowing her disgust.

"Oh, it's just baby mucus. Just a little bit. Right, Amos?"

He dug his half-wiped face into his mother's shoulder before popping a sand-covered finger into his mouth, opening his eyes wide with astonishment and beginning another fresh chorus of howls.

Elsie stalked off. Her baby brother was so different than her baby sisters had been. He pulled cats' tails, got scratched on a regular basis, then sat there and howled exactly like this. The next day he would do it again. He ate dirt, swallowed dimes (Mam found one in his diaper), emptied out cupboards and trash cans, played with shovels and trowels and scissors if he could, and hardly ever played with toys.

Elsie secretly believed there was something seriously wrong with him. He probably had some sort of handicap that wouldn't allow him to go further than third grade. She planned to have a serious talk with her mother about it.

Elsie never understood why her parents couldn't have stopped at four girls. The girl babies had sat in their bouncy seat and played with their toys, or smiled and cooed, blowing little spit bubbles. They also had hair—a nice amount of dark brown fuzz that grew from their scalp like a velvety bonnet, framing their features perfectly. Every one of her younger sisters were good babies—Malinda, Suvilla, and Anna Marie.

Then along came Amos, shattering the well-ordered life of the Esh family. He weighed almost ten pounds and was bald as a volleyball and red as a caramel apple. He never stopped howling unless he slept. So between Elam and Benny being so full of themselves and a baby brother that drove her to distraction, Elsie decided she'd rather not have boys in her world.

Her father wasn't like boys. He was tall and strong and happy, with a shining stainless steel hook protruding from his nearly empty sleeve. It was attached to his shoulder with a series of bands that opened and closed the hook with a rolling motion of his shoulder, so that he could use it like a thumb and a forefinger.

Sometimes he would play games with the little girls, pretending he was the big, bad wolf, snapping the steel hook open and shut like jaws, sending the little girls shrieking up the stairway or into the pantry. He would make awful growling noises as he crept through the house, his back bent double, his head turning from side to side like a hungry predator until even Elsie felt as if she should hide behind the couch.

No, her father was a beloved figure, a whistling person who brought a light into Elsie's world and illumination to all the good things surrounding her she may have missed otherwise. She admired him immensely for the way he soon accepted the loss of his arm, never spoke a word of self-pity, and certainly never turned moody. Sometimes Elsie tucked one arm to her side and kept it there, for hours, just to see how it would feel to be her father. She could pull weeds, but not use a hoe. She couldn't tie the bib apron around her waist, and she certainly couldn't tie her *kopp-duch* under her chin. She couldn't sweep the kitchen, but she could wash dishes, only it took much longer and they weren't too clean.

So who knew, perhaps Amos would grow up to be wonderful like her father someday, but that didn't seem likely.

The house they lived in was close to Gap, a fairly small town in the heavily populated Lancaster County. It didn't seem as if they lived in a bustling area, at home, anyway. The house was built on a rise, among trees, surrounded by farmland. You could barely see Gap off in the distance. At one time, there had been a barn, but a fire had destroyed it in 1937, which was so long ago you'd get tired if you tried to think about it. There was a heap of brown stones, some of them blackened, in a tangle of blackberry vines, thorny as all get out. There were snakes back there, large, slippery-looking black snakes that gave you chills of delicious fright.

The house was actually a farmhouse, but if there was no longer a barn or fields belonging to the house it couldn't be called that. So it was just a house.

Emanuel Lapp owned the two acres of property. He was an older Amish man with a white beard and white hair and more money than President Trump, Elsie decided. He must have, because he owned four farms. He didn't charge them much rent, just enough to let them keep their pride. He hired workers to put on new white siding and new windows with white trim. They cemented the porch floor and added new vinyl posts, which made the house look scrubbed and clean.

Mam planted geraniums and petunias, put in a garden, and trimmed the ancient boxwoods in front of the house. She never complained about cracked linoleum or peeling wallpaper. She put contact paper on the old shelves in the pantry and in the kitchen cupboards, so she could wipe them down with strong Lysol soap. They set their furniture along the walls of the house, painted the steps gray, and lived in it just the way it was.

Sometimes Mam's face would harbor that wistful expression when church was held in some nice home or other. She would run her fingertips along the smooth cupboard doors when no one was watching, or stand in awe of some fancy bathroom done up in a dusty shade of lilac and beige, the shower curtain the identical twin to the window curtain.

But she never mentioned any of it to her husband. How could she? Why hurt his feelings so badly when he was doing the best he could? They had shelter in winter, food to eat, and best of all, each other.

Elsie helped her mother with Amos, washed dishes, and folded laundry. She learned the proper way to hoe, learned how to run the cultivator, and how to pull the small weeds without hurting the vegetable plants or loosening their roots.

She picked peas and beans, shucked corn, picked cucumbers and tomatoes. All summer long, there was the garden, that enormous patch of earth that spilled all kinds of vegetables from the stalks. When April arrived, they ate new spring onions and radishes with fresh homemade bread and butter. When enough warm May sunshine ripened the peas, they bent their backs over endless rows and picked bucketfuls, pouring them into plastic Rubbermaid totes, then sitting on the porch and shelling them for hours. Elsie grumbled and complained, ate raw peas by the handful, and said she didn't know why the minute school let out, the peas were ripe. The truth was, she missed baseball already. What was she supposed to do all summer, with no pony and only long, skinny cats and a screaming baby brother?

They didn't have a trampoline or a swing set. She was too big to play in the sandbox, and besides, that's where the cats did their business. She'd caught them at it. Filthy animals. Cats ran a close second to boys as far as being annoying, but her mother said the cats were here to stay, that the younger girls loved them.

After the peas were all blanched and put in the freezer, the hulls scattered among the peavines for compost in the soil, the green beans and cucumbers got ripe. They brought more backbreaking work, requiring Elsie to bend down and move the beanstalks aside to find the elusive beans hanging underneath.

By the month of June, the sun was hot, hot, hot. Mam did not like the beans to be picked early in the morning when they were wet. Mam's mother always said if you handle the beans when they're wet, they'll get rusty. Whatever she meant by that. How could something become rusty if it wasn't metal? Old wives' tales, Elsie thought, shaking her head. But then, her grandmother was old, so she might have known what she's talking about. Elsie went down to the garden in secret on one dew-filled morning and picked a few handfuls of beans and fed them to the driving horse named George. Sure enough, a week later the next growth of beans was crisscrossed with brown spots. Rusty.

By July and August, Elsie gave up and stopped complaining. The heat was like the roaring furnace in the Bible and the corn and tomatoes and peppers and lima beans were all ready at once. Amos developed a painful-looking heat rash followed by days of loose bowels until his little backside was as red as his face and you could hardly tell which end was which. Mam was constantly in the kitchen, chopping vegetables and mixing vinegar and sugar and pungent spices so that the kitchen took on a sharp, acidic odor, like unwashed underarms. They froze two thousand ears of corn, Elsie told her mother. She laughed, said, "No, no. Now, Elsie. We sold some to the Hoffmeiers down the road."

Mam's face was also a perpetual shade of red. All summer long it stayed that same alarming color, as if the blood vessels beneath her skin were all rising to the surface, ready to explode with tension and heat.

"How old do I have to be before I can get a job?" Elsie asked her father one night, after the sun had left nothing but twilight and a few stars had poked their light through the navy blue curtain of night.

"How old are you now?" he asked.

"Eleven."

"Oh, by the time you're fourteen, you could help Aunt Lydia at market, probably. But remember, Amish children give their wages to their parents. If you make a hundred dollars, you would have only ten to put in your savings account."

He shifted his weight, spun his glass in a circle to

stir the mint tea, then looked at her with an expectant gaze.

Elsie's eyes flashed her irritation.

"If that's the case, I'll never have a pony. Never."

"Elsie, I wish you could have one. But even if ponies were free, we still couldn't afford to feed it. We must be sensible. Lots of children don't have ponies. I never did. Neither did your mother. We grew up to be responsible adults, I like to think."

He smiled at her, that happy, childlike smile that let her know she was loved and everything was right with his whole world.

"But I want a pony."

"Not just a pony," her father replied, "but a cart and a harness and a halter and a lead rope, and enough money to buy two scoops of feed and two blocks of hay. Every day."

"That's right."

Elsie drew up her knees, pulled her skirt tightly around them, then wrapped her hands around her legs, her fingers interlaced. She watched her father's expression, hoping to find his solid reserve crumbling, even a bit.

"Listen. I would love to see you have a pony. But your mother is in dire need of necessities she never mentions. If there is any money left over, ever, we need a new mattress set and a lawn mower that works. They don't require feed and hay. So for now, you'll have to be reasonable."

Elsie knew what he said was true, but that didn't take the sting away. She felt trapped. Even if she worked hard at the market or as a *maud*, she'd never make enough to buy a pony if she had to give so much of the money to her parents. Still, she was determined. She'd figure something out, eventually.

Chapter Two

LUNCH AT SCHOOL WAS ONLY FIFTEEN MIN-
utes, and she stayed at her desk, eating whatever her
mother had packed. She unwrapped her cheese sandwich and ate it quickly, mostly to hide the whole
thing before anyone saw there was no ham or bologna. She never turned sideways in her seat and put
her legs in the aisle to socialize like the other kids did.
They didn't have to see what she got out of her faded
old Coleman lunch box, crisscrossed with scratches
and scruff marks.

"Hey."

Elsie didn't turn, didn't expect to be addressed at
lunch hour.

"Hey, Elsie."

She put back the sandwich, turned and raised her
eyebrows.

"You're not on my team today, are you?"

Now what? Elam never acted as if he cared one
way or another whose team she was on. She knew he

disapproved of her ball-playing abilities, so what did he care?

"I don't know."

"Well, Artie here thinks you're on his team, and he hasn't won a game for so long, he doesn't even know how to be a winner anymore."

Artie was short for Arlen, and Elsie avoided him as much as she could. He came from a wealthy family who lived in a beautiful house about half a mile away. They went to Florida every winter, taking the children for a few weeks and calling it "educational."

"So whose team were you on yesterday?" Elam asked.

"Yours."

He turned to Artie gleefully. "I told you."

That was puzzling. Why would Elam think her being on his team was a good thing?

Elsie shrugged. You could never tell what boys thought. Likely they had some sort of bet going on that she would never find out about.

Elsie's tattered glove was like a shot of caffeine. Pure adrenaline. And it was a perfect day for baseball—barely a breeze, the sun warm but not too warm, the air clear, tinged with the smell of autumn leaves, acorns, dirt, and dying weeds.

She took her place on first base and watched Artie as he walked to the pitcher's space. He had all the confidence in the world, a slight bounce in every step. Rosanne was the catcher. Why they'd put her there was beyond Elsie, seeing how hard it was for her to bend over and stop grounders, given her size. Not that Elsie would ever say that out loud.

Samuel, a fifth-grader, was up to bat and lopped a perfect grounder to Artie, who threw the ball to Elsie. Samuel made a wild lunge for first base, but dropped his shoulders dejectedly when Elsie playfully tagged him.

She smiled. "Nice try."

"Thanks."

Elsie made two home runs, racking up points for the team, caught fastballs on the outfield, and threw with razor precision. No one ever said much to her about her ball-playing abilities, though she got a lot of high fives on the field. The girls seemed almost embarrassed that she was so good—like maybe it wasn't proper to be that much better than all the boys.

Today, Elam grinned at her. "Poor Artie. Whooped 'em."

She smiled back, too shy to speak. She felt the blush in her face, hoped no one would see.

At the end of each school day, Elsie always felt a sense of loss. Going home meant working for her mother at an endless round of weary jobs—getting laundry off the line, sweeping the kitchen, picking up toys, or worst of all, peeling potatoes. She hated plodding around like an ordinary housewife.

Elsie had no plans of becoming a housewife. At twenty-one years of age she could keep the money she earned, all of it. She'd find the hardest, most challenging job she could find and work herself up to manager, maybe running her own stand at the bustling market in New Jersey that Rosanne talked about. Then she would put all of her money into a savings account until she could buy a pony. Just one perfect Shetland pony with an arched neck and shining, well-kept hooves and a shower of light-colored long hair, thick and clean that hung down the side of his neck, a portion of it down the front of his face. She would name the pony Cliff, for the tall hills and ravines of their native country.

The cart would not be painted black, but varnished natural wood with a sheen like water. It would have a red upholstered seat with a comfortable back and red pinstripes on the wheels and along the shafts.

Elsie's daydreaming was what kept her going as she swept the broken linoleum with the scraggly broom, washed the dishes in soapy water, folded cloth diapers, and ironed the Sunday handkerchiefs. Never once had she taken into consideration that at twenty-one she might be too tall, too adult, to be driving a Shetland pony.

Church services were announced to be at their house that Sunday, which meant no one would relax for two whole weeks. It always sent a thrill down her spine, though, to hear her father's name—Levi Esh—announced in church. It was a reminder that they were an upstanding family, capable of hosting services in the garage attached to their house.

Being Amish meant there was no church building with a steeple and pews the way countless English folks enjoyed. You took your turn about once a year, sometimes more, depending on the size of the congregation. Amish folks only went to church every other Sunday, the in-between one meant for Bible study and German lessons with the family, a day of relaxation and rest. Most people went visiting or had company, or went to a neighboring district to church.

Amish families were sectioned into districts, from twenty to forty families in each district. If the congregation grew too large, they would decide on a boundary, dividing the church into smaller sections, which was more manageable to host services. That meant ordaining new ministers, casting lots to select men who were ordained to spread the gospel. This was a sacred thing, and one Elsie didn't fully understand. She had overheard her parents' conversation about how hard it was for Ben Zook, being only twenty-seven years old and so shy and humble. He took it hard when he was chosen, but his wife, Sarah, would be a great help.

In the days leading up to church, Elsie went to school, came home, and worked. She scoured the bathroom and ironed curtains, polished floors and raked leaves. She was old enough now to notice the walls that needed a good cover of paint and the uneven, pockmarked cement floor. There wasn't much she could do about those things, though, and she figured people understood. They knew her family didn't have much money and that it wasn't for lack of hard work or due to frivolous spending.

She helped her mother bake dried-apple pies on the Saturday morning before church services would be held in the garage the following day. First, Mam put the dried-apple *snitz* in a large, sixteen-quart kettle, poured a fair amount of water into it, and set it to boil. Flavored with brown sugar, white sugar, and cinnamon, thickened with granules of minute tapioca, the pie filling was wonderful.

Years ago, dried-apple *snitz* was the way church pies were made, but along the way some enterprising person had proved to have a faster method, using apple butter and applesauce, instead of peeling, slicing, and drying apples, storing them, and cooking them down. It was much easier to dump two gallons of applesauce and one of apple butter and flavor it, and it tasted about the same. But there were many apples in the old orchard, and unwilling to waste any of them, Elsie's mother always picked them up and peeled, sliced, and dried them on an old window screen placed on a rack on the stove. They often wound up with more dried apples than jars of applesauce or apple butter, so they still made *snitz* the traditional way.

Elsie brushed the tops of the crusts with beaten egg, sifted a handful of piecrust crumbs over that, then washed dishes and kept Amos away from the hot stove.

She was secretly proud of her mother's beautiful pies. It took away the sting of not being able to serve sliced ham or bologna, which her parents could not afford. Aunt Mamie was bringing ten dozen red beet eggs and Aunt Annie had said she'd bring a box of seasoned pretzels. The ladies from church would bring cheese spread, peanut butter, and marshmallow spread, loaf after loaf of homemade bread, and cakes and desserts.

Her Saturday was perfect. The weather was beautiful, the air nippy enough that she needed a sweater to mow grass. The leaves were raked and burned, the flower beds cleaned out, the borders cut perfectly with the string trimmer. Windows gleamed after their washing, the siding was free of dust and fly dirt, and the floor of the garage was washed and dried, the carpet laid, and tool shelves covered with old white bedsheets.

Her father set the benches, carrying them in from the racks built into the bench wagon, the large gray homemade enclosures on steel wheels that brought the benches, dishes, and hymnbooks to the home where services would be held. Anna Marie bounced around like a little rabbit, slapping the rows of benches as she dashed between them. Suvilla chased her up and down the long rows till Dat made them stop. It was exciting to host church services, especially for the children.

Elsie leaned into the push mower, down at the lower end of the yard, where the grass was so thick and hard. She had reached the end of the row and turned to lean on her mower handle to catch her breath when she heard the familiar *clip clip clip clip* of a pony's small, light hooves. A horse's feet went slower, and clopped heavily, where a pony's feet moved more quickly, creating a staccato sound.

Just her luck. Here she was, standing beside the road, and here they came, that Elam and his strange little brother, Benny. There was no avoiding the arrogant brothers today. She contemplated diving into the undergrowth beside the yard, but figured they'd already seen her, wearing the bright red dress, black sweater, and white scarf. They couldn't miss her.

She leaned into the mower, without stopping to look or allowing herself the privilege of watching the pony in action.

"Hey!"

She heard the hello, but kept on going, not wanting to give Elam the satisfaction of her longing. She'd never have a pony, so why should he get to look down on where she stood, gazing admiringly at his beautiful Cookie?

"Hey, stop!"

She stopped and glared with what she hoped was an icy look. At least condescending, as in, *Can't you see I'm busy? And it doesn't matter one tittle that you can drive that beautiful pony while I push this clunky old mower around.*

"Elsie."

"What?"

"I'm getting a horse. A paint. Black and white. My dad says I'm too big for a Shetland pony. Ask your dad if you can buy Cookie."

For a moment her heart leaped, but just as quickly reality came crashing back. "Yeah. Well, you know."

"What?"

"We couldn't afford to keep a pony."

"It's that bad?"

Elsie shrugged. "S'what my father says."

"Too bad."

"Yeah."

Benny lifted his face to wipe a trail of mucus from his nose with his coat sleeve.

Elsie swallowed. Gross. *Use a handkerchief,* she thought.

"You look like a red-headed woodpecker," Benny announced, after a second swipe at his streaming nose.

Elam threw back his head and laughed so loudly he sounded like a blue jay. Elsie narrowed her eyes and told Benny she didn't see how he could see at all with that hat over his eyes.

Elam interrupted before Benny could send back another retort. "Well, if I get my horse, bring your sisters to see him. I'll give them a ride with Cookie."

He lifted the reins and moved off without a backward glance.

Elsie watched them go, the up-and-down rhythm of the cart, the pony's hooves hitting the macadam in light, quick succession, then turned back to her mowing.

She would. She'd take her sisters to see his new horse. He'd probably only said it because he pitied them, not because he actually thought they'd come. But why shouldn't she? She didn't want him feeling sorry for her. She was happy and led a good life with loving parents and sweet sisters. Well, there was always Amos, but he couldn't really help how he acted, being only one year old. So Elam could stop pitying her, if that's what he was doing.

Her mother praised her efforts, said the yard looked wonderful, so green and evenly cut, and that she didn't know what she'd do without her help.

"You're so capable, Elsie. Thank you."

Her dat's smile was the sweetest icing on the cake, and Elsie thought no pony could ever mean more to her than her parents' kindness.

The following morning they all got out of bed at five o'clock and ate a hurried breakfast of oatmeal and toast. Then Elsie washed dishes while Mam did the little girls' hair, dressed them in colorful blue dresses with black pinafore-style aprons of black capes and belt aprons, pinned their white coverings on their heads, and told them to sit quietly now, don't go get yourselves all wrinkled and *schtruvvlich*.

Elsie changed Amos's cloth diaper, then dressed him in a little white shirt with a black vest and trousers, attached the hooks to the eyes of the vest front, and told him he looked like Dat.

"Da. Da," he said proudly, marching around the kitchen on short, fat legs.

"Better get your hair done, Elsie," Mam said, glancing at the clock.

So Elsie went to the bathroom, got out the brush and fine-toothed comb, the plastic spritz bottle of water, and set to work. Her hair was heavy—dark brown with a reddish undertone. Mam said it was auburn, but no one else said that. Her round face was tanned, so the smattering of freckles was barely visible. In winter, when the tan faded, the freckles looked like bits of dirt someone had thrown in her face, and stuck. She hated her freckles.

Her eyes were big and green as a dill pickle. She didn't like her eyes, either. She looked a lot like a frog with her eyes so far apart, but there wasn't much you could do about that.

No one ever said anything about her looks, so she had no idea how one went about evaluating oneself. The girls her age in school didn't really include her when they discussed dress fabric or new shoes, where their mothers shopped, or what color their bedrooms were, which was just as well. She didn't have her own bedroom, and her mother never shopped for clothes. As far as she could tell, their clothes were all bought at yard sales or thrift shops, which was fine with her.

She pulled on the fine-toothed comb, drew the heavy tresses back at the desired angle, then clipped the bobby pins on each side. She gathered her hair into an elastic ponytail holder and wrapped it expertly into a bun on the back of her head. A few pumps of water, an overhead shower of hairspray, and Elsie was finished.

She slipped the blue dress over her head and her mother brought the white cape and apron and quickly pinned them in place, muttering about her growth spurt, the apron a good two inches too short. Elsie placed the white covering on her head, and she was ready.

Mam took a second look, a bewildering appraisal that would follow her repeatedly through her days. Mam looked as if she might cry, or laugh. She actually looked a bit hysterical.

"You look nice, Elsie," she said gruffly, and turned away.

She wondered if she did look nice. She even went to the bathroom mirror to check, but she looked the same as she always had.

Fast-stepping horses pulled freshly washed carriages up to the house, dropped off the women and girls, then moved on to the barn, where the men would unhitch and tie the horses to the wooden flatbed wagon her father had set in the barnyard. Blocks of hay were scattered along both sides, so the horses could have a snack after their bridles were removed and comfortable halters slipped over their heads.

Elsie often thought those horses could easily drag that wagon off, a sort of mutiny, a horse rebellion, but they were all docile creatures, well trained and obedient, standing there tethered to the wagon to work till they were untied and led to the carriage, backed between the shafts, and ordered to pull the family home. But that wasn't the only reason she loved horses. They were beautiful creatures with soft, expressive eyes that showed a good spirit, ears that flicked from front to back, and gorgeous flowing manes that rippled the way she imagined prairie grass did, or the ocean waves. "Splendid" was the perfect word to describe a horse.

Elsie filed into church services with the bunch of single girls, quietly, seated by age, the way all Amish girls were traditionally seated. At first, she looked down at her lap, shyness washing over her like a wet shower, but later, after the singing had started, she looked up to find a whole row of ministers, single boys, and young fathers staring at her. Well, they weren't actually staring at her, but it seemed as if they were. Some of the older girls were chewing gum, whispering, or flirting with a few of the bold *rum-schpringa*-aged boys. Most of the girls sat decently, listening to the rising and falling of the preacher's voice.

When they began to sing the last song, Elsie rose and made her way along the long line of girls to help her mother, grandmother, and aunts prepare the food for lunch. They set out fourteen Styrofoam bowls of pickles and fourteen of pickled red beets with the purplish-pink hardboiled eggs nestled among them. There were also seasoned pretzels, spreads, jelly, butter, and pie.

Elsie helped stack towers of homemade bread slices on plates, then turned her back to spread a bit of cheese spread on a crust of bread, quickly gulping it down in a few bites. Breakfast had been a long time ago.

The rest of the day was spent in the company of her cousins, her grandmother Malinda, and all the chattering aunts. Elsie was always genuinely happy to be among them, a part of a growing circle of belonging, new babies and new husbands or wives added every year.

She didn't mind the absence of sliced ham. Not until Rosanne complained about it. The crust of bread stuck in her throat and she coughed and took a drink of water, deeply ashamed.

Elsie heard Rosanne whisper, "We never have ham here. They're poor."

Nothing to do or say about that, so she left it where it belonged. With them.

She figured sliced ham and a pony were no match for kindness, happiness, and contentment, which they had. All three of those things. So much they tumbled out of a container, ran out, and dripped on the tabletop. But you couldn't tell people things like that without sounding boastful.

She had been helping with the tables and had to eat last, with the aunts and mothers. A few boys had not yet eaten, so they were seated at the same table. She found herself next to Elam Stoltzfus, his little brother Benny opposite, hardly recognizable in clean Sunday clothes and without the smashed hat.

Benny sized up his brother with Elsie and said in

a much too loud tone of voice that they looked as if they were getting married, then honked and wheezed at his hilarity, receiving a withering look from Elsie. But from Elam he got a wide grin that pretty much amounted to a home-run high five, which set him to chortling in glee.

Chapter Three

AFTER CHURCH SERVICES WERE HELD IN THE garage, everything was put back in order. Dat worked at putting the benches back into the bench wagon, with Elsie's help. Mam scrubbed floors and dusted, took care of all the leftovers, washed the front porch, and had a long nap with her little ones snuggled by her side.

That Saturday, Elsie and two of her sisters, Malinda and Suvilla, walked over to the Stoltzfus farm. Elsie's desperation to drive a pony overrode any unwillingness she might have had to accept Elam's invitation. It was time she experienced holding the reins, being in charge of the high-stepping pony drawing the lovely cart.

Of course, she'd have to admire the new horse, too, which was annoying. That was all she ever did, it seemed. Admire Elam's horses and his ability to drive them.

Well. Things were about to change.

She marched up to the front door and talked to Elam's mother, who was a good friend of her family, a comfortable, middle-aged woman with spreading hips and a loud voice.

"Yes," she said, "go on out, they're out there in the barn with the horses." Then she handed Malinda and Suvilla lollipops, those big ones with Tootsie rolls inside.

Elam met them at the barn door.

"What's up, Elsie?"

"I came over to see your horse."

"Good. Benny, hitch up Cookie to give the girls a ride."

"Sure. Come this way, girls, you can help me hitch him up. Hey, where'd you get those?" He pointed at the lollipops.

"Your mam," Malinda said quietly.

Elsie followed Elam to a box stall and waited while he opened the gate and led a horse out to the forebay. It was a vision, like a horse from her dreams. It was mostly white, the back a dazzling, glossy black. It had large, gentle eyes, a shapely neck with a small head and curved ears, and a black mane and tail.

Elsie was speechless. She stood and stared at that horse with huge green eyes, her mouth open but no words coming out of it. She wanted to act cool, as if this horse wasn't anything special, she'd seen hundreds just like him, but she couldn't do it.

Finally she said, "He's really nice."

"Right?"

Elsie nodded, dumbfounded.

"You want to ride him? He has a mind of his own. You have to let him know who's in charge."

Elsie shook her head.

"No, I can't ride in a dress."

She waved a hand self-consciously over her skirt.

"My sisters do," Elam said.

"But they probably wear something, don't they? I mean, you know, under their skirt."

"Yeah, they do."

Elsie put a hand on the beautiful paint's neck, slid it slowly to his head, the side of his face. The horse lowered his head, so Elsie stroked the perfect ears, ran her fingers through the long black hair that hung over his forehead. When the horse laid his soft nose against her sweater, she looked at Elam in disbelief.

"He likes me."

Elam grinned. "Looks like it, doesn't it?"

Elsie placed both hands on the horse's face, one on each side, and whispered, "You lovely, lovely creature, you." She glanced at Eli. "What's his name?"

"Haven't named him yet."

"Do you have an idea?"

"I'll think of something."

He didn't ask her for suggestions, so Elsie stepped back as Elam led the horse away. Elsie felt a decided sense of loss and wondered how long it would be before she could touch the satiny neck below the heavy mane again.

She drove Cookie that day. She sat in the driver's seat and held on to the reins with both hands, Elam to her left and Benny sandwiched in between. The feeling of sitting on the upholstered seat, her feet pushed up against the front of the cart for balance, the reins in her hands, the smell of the leather and pony, the up-and-down rhythm of the cart, was beyond description.

Most of all, the ripple of energy that snaked along the reins from the bit in Cookie's mouth was unlike anything she had ever experienced. To turn to the right or left took a slight touch, only a gentle drawing back on either rein. She imagined the tender mouth, the alert, intelligent pony who could feel the modest pressure on the iron bit in his mouth. She kept a steady tension on the reins, turned him perfectly.

That was when the real thrill began.

Sensing he was homeward bound, Cookie's ears pricked forward, his steps increased, and Elsie steadied her hands and applied more pressure.

"Hold him," Elam said evenly.

Elsie bit her lip, didn't answer. She was so intent on doing just that, she barely heard his words. Realizing her hands were not where they should be, she gripped the reins with one hand till she was able to hold them farther out, away from her body, in order to apply all her strength.

Cookie bent his neck, took the bit in his teeth, and ran. His heavy mane flapped up and down, his neck was arched, his ears turned forward, his legs churning as his little hooves pounded the macadam.

Blip, blip, blip—the staccato sound stirred an unnamed emotion in her. She drew her mouth into a straight line, her lower lip caught between her teeth, to stop the shameful tears that came to her eyes.

This was unreal. This was pure, heady joy.

A great love for the spirited little animal welled up until she was afraid her breathing would be stopped.

"Hold him!" Elam yelled.

Elsie didn't answer, just kept up a steady force on the leather reins, her arms extended, her back straight.

Benny yelled something unintelligible from beneath the crushed straw hat, but Elsie stayed quiet, concentrating on driving the energized pony.

There was the Stoltzfuses' driveway. Going at this rate, there was no possible way to make the turn. She used all her remaining strength to slow Cookie, but it was no use.

"Just keep going," Elam said, laughing.

So she did. Soon enough, the pony slowed, and Elsie could turn him around easily, then trot into the driveway at a decent pace. In spite of the diminished speed, the wheels were pulled sideways, scraping a wide arc in the gravel.

To approach the barn contained another sense of

loss. Elsie sat on the cart, reluctant to hand over the reins. But she knew she was being selfish, so she did, without meeting Elam's eyes.

"Thank you," she said quietly.

"You're welcome."

Malinda and Suvilla were given a ride, then it was time to go home. Elsie had a dozen questions to ask, but felt too shy, not wanting to be a pest. So she gathered her little sisters and they thanked Elam again.

"Right-o," he said. Then, "You're a good driver, seeing that was your first time."

Elsie mumbled something unintelligible and left, herding her sisters out the drive and down the road.

After that day, Elsie's passion for horses took on a new intensity. She planned and schemed and connived the best possible approach of acquiring a pony. Or a horse.

She worked hard after school. She mowed the grass for the last time, raked leaves, and washed the porch floor with soapy water and a stiff broom. She walked to the neighboring farm for milk, watched

Amos on Saturdays while her mother went to town for groceries, and never complained about any job, no matter how difficult.

She asked her father again.

"You still haven't given up on a pony?" he asked, laying aside a copy of the newspaper that was thrown in their yard twice a week.

"No."

"We shouldn't have allowed you to go to the boys' place."

"Why?" Elsie asked, already touching the substance of his refusal.

"Well, it certainly didn't help with your pony obsession."

He reached over to retrieve his coffee cup, slurped the hot black liquid, and replaced the cup back on the light stand. "If you'd never driven that pony, you wouldn't know what you're missing. It's just like being Amish and driving a horse and buggy. If you never own a vehicle or learn to drive one, you remain content, and that's as it should be. You know how often I've told you, Elsie—the funds simply aren't available. When you're older, the income you'll bring in for your family will be a welcome boost to the household finances. I can't help my handicap any more than you can help being born into a family like us."

He hesitated. "Not that there's anything wrong with us. We have more than enough—we're rich, compared to many people. I have to give up every morning to having only one hand, and you will have to practice giving up your own will as well. Giving up at a young age is essential to becoming a well-grounded, mature adult. You must learn to be happy without everything you think you can't live without. Material things are not important, Elsie."

Elsie sniffed, toyed with the fringe on the old granny-square afghan that always lay on the arm of the green tufted sofa. Elsie hated that afghan. Mam had dug through the free box at a neighbor's yard sale, pulled it out with shining eyes, and held it up for Elsie to admire in all its hideous, pilled, musty glory.

"But ponies and cars are different. Ponies are allowed," she said, her voice already hushed as she struggled to accept her father's words.

Later, she talked to her mother while they washed dishes.

"Oh, Elsie, do you have any idea how gladly I would give you a pony? I can see it in your eyes, and it hurts to see you standing at the gate, watching Elam and Benny. But what your father tells you is the truth, and hard as it may be, it's better to say no than to try to hand over everything you girls ask for."

"Well, we never ask for anything, so how do you know?" Elsie burst out, and then saw her mam's strained expression and wished she'd kept her mouth shut.

Winter came with a fierce blast of icy Arctic air and gray clouds that churned and boiled above them like woolen sheep. Mam hurried to pull the last of the turnips and carrots, the woodstove in the living room crackled and burned, and the baseball games came to a chilly end.

Standing shivering in the frigid wind and stomping their feet to stay warm took away the thrill of popping flyers and catching grounders. The Ping-Pong table was set up in the middle of the classroom, and serious competition ensued.

Christmas excitement was in the air, especially after the teacher handed out parts for the Christmas program. The pupils giggled behind their copies, raised hands, and asked dozens of questions until the harried teacher became red-faced and impatient, snapping at her overenthused troupe and efficiently deflating the Christmas spirit.

Elsie walked home from school, her Christmas poem in her lunch box, her head down, her feet shuffling. Ahead of her, Malinda raced in circles with her friends, not yet touched by the burden of being poor, of being different than everyone else.

Elsie dreaded Christmastime. With each passing year, it got worse. Eating her cheese sandwich, listening to the upper grades chattering on about their wish lists, the shopping, the wrapping and gift giving, the final blow the tallying of mounds of different items they received. Of course, Elsie never participated.

She imagined herself seated beside Rosanne and Lydia Mae, talking about her new pony named Dream, or the coat her mother had found at Target. What was Target? She had no idea. At least there was a big meal to look forward to. There was always *roasht*, mashed potatoes, candied carrots, and homemade noodles with plenty of rich brown gravy. There were cookies and homemade candy, Rice Krispies treats, peanut butter fudge, and chocolate-covered peanuts and raisins. But they each received only one gift—a doll or a pair of warm slippers. Never both.

And so when Christmastime came, Elsie caved inward, became quieter and more reserved. She was who she was, and accepted it, but it still rankled at times, like a burr stuck in her sock. You suffered the itch until you took the time to reach down and extract it, which was actually a whole lot easier than extracting this jealousy, or whatever you called it when you stood on the sidelines and knew you amounted to the grand total of zero.

By the time Elsie had completed eighth grade and had been given a diploma saying she had successfully passed to vocational class, she had driven Cookie a number of times, but never came close to acquiring a horse of her own.

Elam became different, then.

He didn't help her hitch up Cookie anymore. Benny did. Elam was always busy on the farm. He never looked at her anymore, either, just sort of swung his gaze behind her head and looked at whatever was back there. He blushed. Furiously. His face turned dark red and he blinked so rapidly he hardly knew what to do.

That was a mysterious thing to Elsie, but she figured he pitied her for not being able to have a pony and didn't know what to do about it. Boys were like that. She had observed this phenomenon many times, watching them get softhearted with sympathy or admiration and covering it all up with a hard exterior.

So she didn't think about it much, just let Elam go his way, and she went hers.

Benny became her funny little friend, though. He didn't try to be funny, he just was. He hardly ever took that straw hat off, even in winter. The brim had torn along the crown, from Benny yanking on it so much, so when it was really windy, the front of his hat would be blown straight up, which acted like a sail and tugged even harder, causing Benny to run around the farm with one hand smashed down on top of his head.

When Elsie turned fifteen, she was through vocational class and ready to look for a job. She had four options: working at the market, helping at one of the many local dry-goods stores, housecleaning for English ladies, or being *maud* to Amish housewives who had a new baby, were housecleaning, or simply needed an extra hand at canning or freezing the garden produce. Elsie shrewdly calculated hours, the price paid per hour, and how many days her mother would allow her to work. Though housecleaning paid the most per hour, working at the market would bring in the most money, since the days were long.

So her mother called Amish market stand owners until she procured Elsie a job at the Reading Terminal Market, a place teeming with city folks and hundreds of vendors hawking their goods inside an old railroad station converted to a farmers' market. She would be working for Eli Beiler, starting at a hundred dollars a day, being picked up at 4:00 a.m. Sharp. "She has to be ready,"

Eli had said. "If we stop two minutes at everyone's house we lose fifteen to twenty minutes to get to market. Can't do that."

That scared Elsie. She pictured a king on his throne. A slave owner on horseback holding a whip in one hand.

Her mother hitched the old horse to the buggy and they went to the fabric store to buy cloth for three new dresses. She dug through the large cardboard box on the porch that was marked "Clearance" with a fluorescent yellow sign. Some of the fabric just wasn't selling well; most had a bit of a flaw imprinted into the weave or a few snags.

Mam picked up a bolt of blue fabric with tiny checks in it.

"It's a little fancy," she mused, "but at this price . . ."

Elsie shrugged. She was glad for the new clothes, but would have preferred to use every bit of extra money toward a pony.

"Do you like this?" her mother asked, holding up a bolt of green with a puckered surface.

Elsie gave a noncommittal nod. "Whatever you think. I'm going to look at books."

Mam chose plain white fabric for two new bib aprons, saying her dresses all had a bit of a pattern in them so they'd have to be toned down a bit with the white aprons.

Elsie shrugged again. If she was honest with herself, it wasn't just that she'd rather spend the money on a pony. The thing was, most girls wore pretty new dresses, hoping to get the attention of some boy or to impress the other girls, even if they didn't admit it. She knew she wasn't going be popular, whether she had a fancy new dress or not. Especially now that school was over and she hardly ever saw the other kids her age. She intended to spend as much of her time working as she possibly could—not socializing, and especially not with boys. Elam was the only friend she cared about as far as boys went, but he had turned into an awkward, pimply, blushing creature she couldn't begin to understand, so that was that.

She picked up a romance novel with a horse on the cover and turned it over. $13.99. She read the paragraph on the back, was stabbed with intense longing, but placed it back on the shelf. You could get all kinds of books at yard sales for a quarter, fifty cents, or a dollar. Mam rejected every one that looked vaguely intriguing, said they weren't fit. None of her girls were ever going to fill their heads with that romance stuff. It wasn't true, anyhow.

That left Elsie to wonder how much her mother felt slighted by her father's mishap. Or maybe she had just let love and romance wither and die, leaving only bitterness and a sour attitude.

But no. Her mother and father sincerely loved each other. There was too much happiness and love in their house to think such thoughts. Her parents truly loved each other, no doubt. So with books, like horses, Elsie gave up. She obeyed, didn't question, stayed within the boundaries her parents set for her.

Mam sewed the three dresses, allowing Elsie to sew the top of one, the least expensive. Elsie found it frustrating, setting the sleeves properly, learning to sew in a straight line, but with her mother's encouragement, she didn't do too badly. The bib aprons were harder, so Mam sewed them herself, pressed them, and let Elsie slide one over her head and tie it behind her back.

Elsie stood back, turned slowly for her mother's benefit.

"All right."

That was all she said.

Just all right.

Elsie thought she looked at her with a strange light in her eyes, but that was probably from bending over the sewing machine all day.

She was surprised when her mother came into her bedroom after the lamp was already extinguished. She carried a small battery lamp, her old, faded housecoat swishing as she moved across the floor.

"Elsie."

"Hmm?"

"I want you to be aware of yourself at market. Not all men are honorable. Some might do you harm by wanting you the way a man is not supposed to want a young girl. Here is a book for you to read. It's about how to conduct yourself in a Christian way when you're out in public. You have grown up in the past year, so I think you need to be aware of the proper behavior for a young girl."

With that, she left the room, closing the door softly behind her.

Obediently, Elsie read the thin booklet. It changed

her life forever. She was so deeply shaken she read her *Black Beauty* book for an hour before falling into a restless half sleep that left her tired and irritable in the morning.

When her mother asked if she had read the book, she threw a withering look in her direction and went to the washhouse to begin sorting dirty laundry.

Chapter Four

AND SO ELSIE ENTERED THE VAST, BEWILDER-
ing world of the farmers' market, thrust into an
atmosphere of hustle and bustle, a fast-paced energy
that carried her in its unwilling arms and spilled her
on the cracked cement floor, struggling heroically to
maintain a smidgen of composure.

She knew nothing of piecrusts and rising yeast rolls.
Eli Beiler said they would train her. Ha. The "training" composed of being yelled at by a fat, domineering
woman with thin black hair, a unibrow, and, perched
on a sausage nose, heavy glasses with lenses so thick
they made her eyes appear like little black marbles.

She was vast. Huge. Her white bib apron was so
tight the strings that were knotted around her waist
were completely hidden in rolls of flesh. They called
her Rache, as if she was too busy to finish pronounc-
ing her name. If you tried to call her Rachel, she'd be
through the swinging doors before you could say the
last syllable.

Elsie was given a recipe, a few basic instructions on the mechanics of a huge electric mixer, introduced to a girl named Lillian, and told to take a fifteen-minute break at ten o'clock.

Lillian was short, blond, and almost as loud as Rache. She was also extremely fancy, wearing a pink dress with tight sleeves and a hem that scraped the soles of her shoes. She talked nonstop, chewed gum and snapped it with regularity, drank Pepsi from a plastic cup filled with ice, and ran around on her Nike-clad feet, darting everywhere like an anxious bee.

"OK, here. This is what you do. You dump this out, like this."

She was interrupted by a screech from the mountainous Rache.

"Lillian, stop doing everything for her. She'll never learn. Elsie, here, step up and get that pile of dough onto the kneading table. Lillian, step back, there."

So Elsie dumped, heaved, and learned by bitter trial and error. Lillian was basically very kind, she was just so terribly speedy and outspoken. Rache grumbled all day about being stuck training these new ones, Eli sending them in as innocent as babies.

She eyed Elsie and asked who named daughters that anymore. Poor thing.

Kindhearted Lillian took up for her, said Elsie was old-fashioned, it was cool. "I'll call you Els."

Rache snorted and popped half a custard-filled doughnut in her mouth.

"Elsie, don't wad that dough up like that. These are dinner rolls, so they have to be handled lightly. Use more of that oil spray. These rolls will stick to the pan if you don't."

Elsie was lightheaded with hunger and fatigue by lunchtime. Her ten o'clock break had consisted of hiding in the bathroom for fifteen minutes, ashamed to let anyone in that bakery know she didn't have money to buy snacks. Mam had said she could eat bakery items, but she was too shy to ask for a dough-nut or a whoopee pie. Lillian brought back a few bites of a cheeseburger and some limp fries with wet ketchup stains on them.

"You want this? I'm full."

"You sure?"

Nothing had ever tasted quite as good as those soggy fries and that tepid burger.

All day they mixed, kneaded, shaped, and baked bread, dinner rolls, sandwich rolls, and sticky buns.

Rache yelled at them about the size of the sandwich rolls. "Who was shaping these? Elsie, you need to use more dough."

Not once did Elsie venture into the crowded aisle ways. It seemed like a human stampede, a place where all manner of humanity would walk all over you, crushing you in the process.

She had nothing to eat all day, except the few bites of Lillian's leftover food. She rode home in the back seat of the fifteen-passenger van, crossed her arms over her empty stomach, and didn't talk to anyone.

She burst into tears the moment she spied her mother's face, the story of that awful day coming out in bits and pieces.

"Ach my, Elsie. I had no idea. I am so sorry. Here, sit down."

Elsie shook her head, blew her nose, said she wanted a long, hot bath first. When she returned, her hair dark and wet and wavy, the fine dark smudges of

fatigue below her large eyes, the freckles like a con-
stellation of beauty dust, her mother kept the astonishment at her daughter's budding young beauty to
herself.

She ate a steaming bowl of vegetable soup with
saltines and applesauce, a thick grilled cheese sandwich made with Velveeta cheese and margarine, and
sliced peaches and ginger cake for dessert. Then she
handed her mother a fifty-dollar bill, two twenties,
and a ten. The sensation of gratitude was an unspo-
ken pact.

"Here is your ten dollars, Elsie."

She folded it and put it in the small cedar chest
with the horse painted on the lid. She received five
more dollars to buy food the next day at the market, then went to bed and slept so deeply her alarm
clock's jangling threw her rudely into a strange and
alien world.

The second day at Beiler's Bakery was no worse than
the first, but didn't prove to be much better, either.
She accidentally dropped a heavy plastic dishpan of
dough, which set Rache to yelping like a frightened

puppy. She came at them like a steaming locomotive, saying she couldn't put up with any of this nonsense, she had too much on her mind.

"You mean your hips," muttered Lillian.

Elsie caught her eye and grinned.

At lunch she realized she'd have to brave the crowded aisles to buy food. She stepped out timidly, staying near the wall as much as possible, and bought a hot dog and a drink, plus a bag of potato chips, all for $2.50. She would pocket the remaining money and add it to her savings. She was given an apple by the white-bearded Amish man at the produce stand and a chocolate cupcake by Eli Beiler himself.

He asked how her day was going.

"All right. OK, I guess."

"Good." And he was off.

He didn't care, Elsie reminded herself from time to time. Neither did Rache or Anna or Judy, the English lady who sat at the cash register. In the world of profit and sales, it was each man to himself. Or each girl. So Elsie learned not to expect praise, to be seen without being noticed, to work hard and do her best, just like at school.

Lillian helped her comb her hair to complement her face. She told her she could actually be very pretty if she learned a few things.

"You have gorgeous eyes. You should let me shape your eyebrows."

Elsie was horrified. She had never heard of such a thing.

"You just pull out some of those stray hairs from your eyebrows."

Mam noticed the hair immediately.

"Elsie, how you comb your hair! Now, this is not *alaubt*. Absolutely no way will any girl of mine comb her hair like that. You look awfully worldly. Now you go upstairs and roll your hair back the way I have always taught you. Now go."

Mam fussed. Dat's eyes twinkled at her in a happy, dancing way, so she knew her father understood what it was like to be young and wanting to be a part of something. What it was exactly, Elsie could not be sure, but it was there. A possibility. A tentative knowledge that she would not always be the lone girl who said nothing as she ate her cheese sandwich hurriedly, before the others could see the cheese and homemade bread.

As the weeks turned into months, Elsie's little bundle of money grew. Twenty dollars a week for twenty-four weeks amounted to over four hundred dollars. She had spent some on new coverings and a new pair of sneakers that Lillian bought for her when she went to Rockvale Square, a place Elsie had never seen.

So by the time her sixteenth birthday was a month away, Elsie was one of the best workers the bakery had ever hired and was fast friends with Lillian, who was planning on introducing her to her set of youth. Lillian had taken it upon herself to coach Elsie into popularity, telling her she needed to buy a new pattern for her dresses and redecorate her bedroom, that she should smile when a cute boy came to the stand, and that she needed a particular cream to clear up the occasional blemish that appeared on her jawline.

Sometimes it irked Elsie. She would never fit in, whether she smiled at the right moments and spent all her savings on new things or not. She didn't even have her own room. How was she supposed to redecorate it? She had never chosen her bedroom color or the furniture and she would never ever be allowed to go away in cars with other youth on Saturday evenings. Lillian had taken over her life, telling her what was cool, how to dress, how to act, what to say and think and do, as if programming a robotic person.

She spoke to her parents, who said there was nothing wrong with Lillian, that they just were not quite on the same level. They knew Lillian's parents, in fact. Mam had gone to school with her father. But they had always hoped Elsie would join the group that most of the church girls belonged to, which was not the same group that Lillian went to.

Elsie didn't particularly want to go to Lillian's group, but she also didn't want to disappoint her one friend. She agonized over standing her ground, telling Lillian she would be joining the more moderate group of youth.

She wasn't sure she wanted to join either group, really, but she supposed she'd have to eventually. Part of it was that admitting she was old enough to join the other youth meant admitting she was too old for a pony. It didn't seem fair that she had outgrown her childhood dream without ever having had the chance to own even a cheap, old little pony she could hitch to the express wagon. It seemed to her as if the best years of her life were gone, the rides with Benny and Cookie and her sisters only a memory.

It probably wouldn't be long before Benny started blushing and disappearing right off the face of the earth, the way Elam had. Boys were as strange as they'd ever been.

All you had to do was watch Amos, and you'd know boys were strange and disturbing creatures. Amos cut earthworms with his little sand trowel and ran after the skinny barn cats screeching like a mountain lion. He ate raw beans from the garden like a guilty little rabbit, his nose twitching with pleasure, but if you tried to get him to eat cooked vegetables with mashed potatoes, he threw himself back against his highchair and pounded the footrest with his heels. He wasn't even close to potty trained, and it was disastrous every time Mam made a feeble attempt at achieving it.

"He needs a brother," Dat said.

"He needs discipline," Mam said.

Amos said he didn't want a brother, and he didn't want that other thing, either.

Everyone laughed, which set Amos into all kinds of ungainly antics, until he wore himself out and sat on the couch with his hands clasped in his lap, breathing hard.

A few weeks before Elsie's sixteenth birthday, Lillian bounced into the bakery and announced the fact that Jason Riehl had asked her for a date on Saturday evening. Her face was flushed and her eyes shone as she accepted everyone's congratulations.

Suddenly she turned to Elsie, her smile fading. "Sorry, Els. Since I'll be dating, I guess I can't bring you to my group."

Elsie couldn't have been more relieved.

"That's OK, Lillian. I'm . . . eh . . . joining the group my friends at church go to. I just hadn't told you yet."

"Oh, great! Wonderful. That's good."

Elsie was thoroughly hugged, wished the best.

Rache lumbered in with a shipment of yeast. "What's this I hear?"

"I have a date! With Jason. Jason Fisher."

"Who's he?"

"You wouldn't know."

And with that, the day swung into motion. By now Elsie was so accustomed to the mixer, the dough, the time to bake rolls and bread, it seemed as if she could do it with her eyes closed. The bakery was her friend now, her supporter of dreams. She figured by the time she was eighteen years of age she'd have a few thousand dollars, which would enable her to purchase a horse. A riding horse. Then she'd have to pay for the feed.

She hummed as she worked and smiled at Lillian as she relived the evening of the big question. It seemed like she'd been waiting for ages for Jason to ask her, and now he had.

"Well, I don't want a boyfriend," Elsie said, feeling more confident. "I want a horse."

Lillian's mouth fell open. "A horse? Seriously? What for?"

"I love horses."

"You love horses. Hm. That's different for a sixteen-year-old. I mean, isn't it? If you were English you could ride competitively, like girls doing the barrel-racing thing. Hey, did you ever go to that horse thing in Harrisburg? You know, I think it's in February."

Elsie shook her head, then left to bring another fifty-pound bag of flour from storage. Lillian had no clue. Their lifestyles were so completely different, you could hardly begin to compare the vast underlying separateness of their everyday existence. If Lillian guessed that Elsie's family didn't have much extra, it wasn't because Elsie had said anything. She had learned in school to say nothing, to listen, to show happiness for others.

But being sixteen would hold its own new challenges. Elsie could not be expected to compete with any of the other girls. Things like dresses, sweaters, coats, shoes and purses, money to pay drivers or purchase Christmas gifts or wedding presents would have to come out of the amount she was saving for a horse. The horse was far more important than any number of dresses or shoes, she confided to her mother, who responded with raised eyebrows, an incredulous expression.

"But, Elsie, how do you expect us to pay for all your needs? Surely you want your room painted, with new curtains? I thought perhaps we could find some decent furniture at an estate sale, or a moving sale. Suvilla can move in with Malinda. They won't mind sharing a room. And you'll need new dresses, of course."

"I don't care about that stuff."

And she didn't.

Elsie insisted that they not celebrate her sixteenth birthday. It would simply cost too much to buy that enormous cake and gallons of ice cream. She knew her parents murmured in the living room, each one on their old recliner, reading and relaxing before they retired for the night. Both of them thought it inappropriate, this refusal to enter her years of *rumschpringa* without the traditional party, but Elsie remained adamant.

Shortly after her birthday, she received a substantial raise from Eli Beiler. He told her she was carrying the workload of two girls. Elsie blushed furiously, her gaze fastened on her worn thrift-shop sneakers, having no idea how highly Eli Beiler thought of her.

Here was a rare girl. She deserved every penny of the large raise. It wasn't just the fact that she was a hard worker, it was the efficiency of her movements, her quiet, friendly demeanor, her conscientious fifteen-minute breaks that meant she always appeared back at her workplace a few minutes before it was time to start.

She had even won over Rache, which was no small feat. He had often fancied getting rid of Rache, but knew she was indispensable. He needed her to help manage the place, especially the ordering and distributing.

Elsie told her parents about the raise and offered them the amount she had received. In the end, they allowed Elsie to keep thirty dollars instead of twenty, which they declared only reasonable, seeing how she had pleased her boss, been a good example.

"You have truly honored your father and mother," they told her. Now there was thirty dollars. Twenty for the horse, and ten for what she was slowly accepting as necessities for teenagers.

So, at the urging of her mother, Elsie went to the thrift store in Strasburg. She had no idea what color she wanted the walls of her room painted and couldn't have cared less about curtains or any kind of bedspread, quilt, or comforter. Why spend money on things no one would see, things she didn't care about? But she accommodated her mother, agreed to the packaged quilt and shams (what were shams?), and watched a small child throw a temper tantrum about a Ziplock bag containing small items her mother did not allow her to have, while her own mother chose filmy white curtains yellowed with age, mumbling to herself about homemade lye soap and the power to turn anything snowy white.

They left with bags of good items and went to the paint store, where she paid far too much for one gallon of paint the color of a horse's muzzle—the part that was velvet. She swallowed her annoyance at the expense, knowing this decorating brought her mother more pleasure than herself, definitely. And she couldn't take this away from her.

They painted the walls and gave the old woodwork a fresh coat of white. Mam said it didn't matter if the paint was left over from painting the porch posts and said "Exterior" on the side of the plastic five-gallon bucket.

As they worked, her mother gave her sage advice, talking in a breathless tone as she plied the roller. There were many things to learn about *rumschpringa*, she said, stopping to look into her daughter's eyes.

"Things have changed since your father and I ran around. You will belong to a supervised group, where you won't have to worry about some of the improper behavior that used to be tolerated. Well, not really tolerated—there was plenty of concern, sadness, whatever, but no one really knew what to do about the low morals that had crept in over the years."

"So how did things change?"

"Well, a group of parents and ministers took it on themselves to make a change. And you know how hard it is to do that among our people." She shook her head, rolling her paint roller up and down the corrugated roller pan. "But change has come. There are still plenty of *ungehorsam*, but I think this group is a good one. They're decent kids who care about their future, who seemingly want what is right. So when the time comes to begin dating, I want you to think deeply, pray that God will lead you in the path of righteousness. For one thing, you will be expected to spend your evenings in the living room with your chappy, and not upstairs, the way we did."

"Stop saying 'chappy,'" Elsie said.

Her mother laughed, a deep, happy sound that always made Elsie laugh with her.

"Oh, well, that's what we used to say."

"I know. Don't worry about a chappy for me, Mam. I have no intentions of becoming interested in any young man in the near future. Or the far-away future. I want to keep working until I can get a horse and be able to buy feed and hay, a saddle, and a bridle."

Her mother looked doubtful, but she couldn't help but notice the way Elsie's eyes shone as she talked about her long-held dream.

Chapter Five

BY THE TIME ELSIE REACHED HER SEVENteenth birthday, she had learned the ins and outs of *rumschpringa*, the do's and don'ts, why there were popular girls and girls who were not. She learned to avoid eagerly amorous suitors, too.

Already, she had been "asked" by more than one nervous, bright-eyed young man awash in thoughts of romance, wanting her for their girl. She felt cold-hearted, cruel, but knew it wouldn't work. She simply had no interest in any of them and was rather perplexed that they had an interest in her. She had no idea of her outstanding beauty, her grace and charm.

She understood the girls' room thing now. Her friends spent many hours visiting each other, sitting on the bed, happily gossiping, giggling, dressing up. She enjoyed the time together, reveling in friendship, the kind that brightens existence for each other. And her bedroom was pretty—everyone said so.

"Where did you get this unique furniture?"

"It's really lovely."

Her parents had acquired the furniture at an estate sale, a dull brown thing without a headboard for the bed, a mirror that was broken, and drawer pulls that were so loose they came off in her hand. Her father measured and adjusted, fixed and nailed things together, while her mother applied layers of white primer and paint and glaze. The results were amazing. Her parents did not tell her the weeks of penny-pinching that followed, but she knew, and loved her parents even more.

They made this sacrifice for her.

She was in the garden when he stopped his horse, slid the buggy door aside, and said hello.

Elsie straightened, wiped the back of her hand across her forehead, leaving a brown smudge, and smiled.

Elam. All grown up now, his hair cut fashionably, wearing a white polo shirt and no suspenders, his shoulders wide, his face tanned and chiseled, his eyes deep and dark. Elsie noticed all this fleetingly, her eyes going to the magnificent horse hitched to his buggy—black, huge, and powerful, the neck thick and arched, with a wavy mane that rippled in the evening sun. The horse's feet had long fur around the hooves, in the back, so that his graceful legs looked as if he wore boots.

He stood at attention, his head held high, both front hooves aligned perfectly, his ears flicking, swiveling easily, alert for a command from his master.

Elsie's mouth formed an O of admiration, but there were no words.

"You still looking for a horse?"

Dumbly, she nodded.

"I think I know of someone who has one for you."

"Serious?"

"I think so."

"Where is he?"

"It's a ways off. I thought maybe you'd enjoy a ride over to see him."

Elsie nodded. "When?"

"How about Friday night?"

"You mean, with . . . ?"

She could only incline her head in the direction of the horse hitched to his carriage.

"Yeah, this one can travel twenty miles without becoming winded. His stamina is amazing."

Almost, she echoed him, saying, "He's more than amazing!" But she was certain Elam knew what he was driving, so why gush and exclaim unnecessarily?

"You'll go?" he asked.

"Yes. I certainly will."

"OK. I'll pick you up around five."

She didn't get home from market till seven. It would be too late.

"Uh, I'm sorry. I don't get home till seven."

"How about Saturday night, then? Five?"

"I could do that."

"Good. I'll see you then."

He tugged slightly on the reins and the horse lifted his feet with perfect fluid grace. The steel rims of the buggy wheels moved, crunched on gravel, and he was gone, the gray buggy top, the black underside and wheels with the slow-moving vehicle emblem and row of reflectors shining in the sun.

Elsie turned back to her hoeing, wondering how he knew she still wanted a horse. After school was over, they had parted ways, in every sense of the word. He worked on a construction crew, had joined another youth group, and hardly ever attended church services, likely going to church with buddies who were in other districts.

But he must have remembered.

She bent down to retrieve a long-rooted dandelion from among the cabbages, wondering what had become of Benny. Certainly, the straw hat would be gone from his head, as he approached the age where young men thought about their appearance. Who knew, though? He might still be wearing a hat below his eyebrows, squinting at the world with his altered eyesight.

Elsie smiled to herself, then began humming.

Was it possible her dream may be coming true? A real live horse. Elam had not elaborated on the breed, the place, or anything, really.

She pictured a stable. One of those huge, standing-seam, metal-roofed barns with siding stained to a cheerful yellow-brown color that resembled logs, huge paddocks and riding arenas, a lush pasture dotted with excellent horses. Equine paradise.

Elam would know a good horse when he saw one, so there was no sense in worrying if the animal would be appropriate.

Perhaps, if she was lucky, she'd have money left over for a used saddle and bridle. She thought of the beautiful hues of color on the Navajo-inspired saddle blankets thrown in heaps at the harness shop in Gordonville. To own one of them would be a stroke of good fortune. She loved to follow her father to this shop, the odor of leather and dye, oil and horses, the air sharp with the smell of new nylon ropes and halters. Even as a small child, she had followed her father into the dim interior and stood mesmerized, tracing a design on a brand-new saddle with a forefinger, stepping up as close as possible to the layers of leather harnesses and sniffing deeply. The bio-plastic harness had no smell, which was quite sad, but Dat said they were lighter, better.

Elsie didn't agree, but never said so.

Her anticipation mounted as the days went by. Friday seemed so far off. Lillian was preoccupied, grouchy, if it came right down to it, so there was no happy banter, no Jason this and Jason that. At least Lillian's happy prattle made the day pass swiftly, every week. Finally, Elsie told herself to stop watching the clock. If she checked every fifteen minutes it seemed as if the day would never end.

Rache lumbered into the yeast bread corner, carrying a handful of silver trays.

"Hey you, Lillian. Elsie, that last batch of hamburger rolls was too small. I mean, the rolls. You have to stop skimping on the dough. That's not going to help our sales."

When there was no answer, she cleared her throat.

"Just so you know."

Then she turned on her heel and moved away.

"Good. You didn't talk to her, either," Lillian commented.

"I couldn't think of anything to say. I guess they were too small."

"Puh. She isn't happy if she doesn't pick on someone."

And so Elsie picked up speed, tried to correct the problem, and stopped watching the clock. In spite of her best efforts, the day seemed endless. Her shoulders ached, her feet hurt, and she was upset at Lillian.

Saturday was even worse.

Finally, she found her coworker in a corner, her back turned, wiping her eyes with a crumpled Kleenex, her nose red and swollen.

Without thinking, Elsie slipped an arm around her waist, and whispered, "What's wrong, Lillian?"

Without answering, Lillian tore away from her, knocking down a pyramid of bread pans that clattered to the floor, creating a sound that brought Rache immediately.

"Seriously, Lillian," she said, in a low, threatening voice.

Red-faced and flustered, Lillian bent to gather up the pans, keeping her face averted without giving Rache the satisfaction of a reply.

"Try not to let that happen again."

Lillian straightened, her eyes shooting sparks of outrage.

"It was an accident, OK? So go mind your own business." Then she muttered "Fat cow" under her breath, or what she hoped was under her breath, but

Rache caught the nasty slur and went crying to Eli
Beiler, and Lillian was let go that day.

Fired.

Elsie was horrified. She felt awful about Lillian
and worried for herself. To be fired from her job
would be complete annihilation of her dream. A
popped balloon.

She couldn't afford to be in ill spirits and must
certainly never vent her feelings about a coworker.
She must pay close attention to details. If there was
no market job, there was no horse.

The thing was, Rache was indispensable. She was
the queen of the bakery. So there was no use denying
her superior position, or fighting against it. Elsie felt
a stab of pity for Lillian, her unnamed troubles, and
the stinging humiliation of being fired.

Rache confided in her, then. It wasn't just the
slur; Lillian had been slacking off in her duties, which
Elsie was carrying, until she was easily doing three
fourths of everything, and it wasn't fair.

Rache sat down, braced her tired back with her
palms clipping her knees, a cup of cappuccino at her
elbow, and said she had been trying to get her niece

to take Lillian's place for a while already, but wasn't having any luck.

"She isn't interested." She sighed, took a sip of her hot drink, grimaced, pried the lid off, and blew across the top. "Hot, hot, hot," she said.

"Do you have anyone in mind?" she asked, after swirling a mouthful like Listerine mouthwash, then bending for another slurp, more grimacing.

"Perhaps my sister Malinda. She's not sixteen yet."

"You have a sister? Perfect. I'm going to tell Eli. Oh, here. Here he is. Eli!" she bellowed, wagging a finger like a rope sausage. When he appeared, Rache pointed at Elsie.

"She has a sister. Could we hire her?"

Eli whistled, low. "I would say so."

Elsie nodded, said she'd bring her along the following week.

Her parents agreed immediately. But Malinda smiled, shook her head, and said no, she didn't think she'd enjoy bakery work, but thanks for asking. That brought one raised eyebrow from Dat, pursed lips from her mother. After a brief discussion, Malinda agreed to go.

Not that she did so without complaining to Elsie, though.

By the time Saturday evening came, Elsie stopped thinking about the bakery and Malinda's coming introduction to all of Elsie's own trials and mistakes, and focused entirely on the upcoming ride to an undisclosed location with Elam Stoltzfus.

She didn't worry about the color of her dress and had no time to fuss with her hair and covering, having arrived home only thirty minutes before five. She didn't think Elam would notice her appearance. He was merely doing this to help her find the long-awaited horse, which was thoughtful and very kind.

She gasped when he drove in, sure she felt like any English girl if someone had picked her up in a very expensive, foreign-made car, one you seldom saw and, of course, never had the opportunity to drive.

The horse bounced, all grace and strength, lifting his front hooves high, his neck proud and powerful. The buggy wheels flashed as if there were water on the spokes, the gray canvas top flawless.

Nervous now, Elsie smoothed a palm down the front of her black apron, inhaled a steadying breath, told her mother goodbye, and walked through the door, down the steps along the cracked, uneven sidewalk.

Elam sat in the buggy and watched her descend the porch steps, wondering how Elsie seemed never to notice how perfect she was. She was as fresh as an April shower, and as invigorating.

When she slid in beside him, he looked into her eyes once, then found himself immediately tongue-tied, all the clever words he had planned on saying evaporated like steam off the apple butter kettle.

"Where are we going?" she asked eagerly.

"North of Ephrata."

"Way up there?"

He nodded, could not think of one word to say. They rode side by side, too close, yet too far away, in an uncomfortable silence. Elam was dry-mouthed, horrified. He tried to remind himself that this was Elsie—the expert ballplayer who was tall and skinny, put in the background by the other girls. He'd known her most of his life.

Elsie was too shy to lead the conversation. This was Elam Stoltzfus, the Elam of good fortune, who owned ponies and horses and never allowed her to drive. Or hardly ever. He was so far above her in everything—knowledge, prestige, wealth, a good, solid name in the community, and now, very, very good-looking.

She leaned against the soft seat back, crossed her arms, and relaxed. If he didn't talk, then there was no reason to become upset. Besides, she could sit and watch the black horse run for miles and be content.

The buggy seemed light, like an afterthought to the horse, or as if it had never been there in the first place. This horse ran for the joy of running, creating a flowing motion where the buggy seemed to be a part of the horse.

Elsie couldn't help but compare him with the only tired old Standardbred they owned. He trotted along with his loose ungainly pace, creating a jerking motion as soon as the road inclined, then slowed to a walk, which resulted in being tapped with the tip of the frayed old whip. As soon as he felt the whip, he jumped, lunged into his collar, only to slow to another walk a bit farther down the road.

This created plenty of movement, being jerked forward then slammed back against the seat, the seat itself lifting a bit from time to time.

"So, what do you do?" Elam croaked finally, then grimaced inwardly with the pain of the lame attempt.

"Do? You mean, as in work?" she asked, her voice low.

He nodded, too miserable to search for further words. What was wrong with him? He felt beads of perspiration form on his forehead, but was far too embarrassed to lift his left hip to fumble for his handkerchief. As long as she didn't look in his direction, he'd be all right.

"I work at the Reading Terminal Market. In the bakery."

"Do you like it?" Oh my. See Jane run. Run, Sally, run. His words were completely predictable, as if he'd read them from a first-grade reading book. He cringed, sniffed with misery.

"I do, actually. I like my boss, Eli Beiler from the Cattail area. Do you know him?"

"I don't believe I do." Whew. That cliff-hanger was done. Now what was he going to come up with?

The long ride was turning into an excruciating form of mental endurance. He had always prided himself on being the suave conversationalist with all the girls he knew, so this shake-up had not been foreseen. Ill-prepared to meet an unexpected rush of awe, never associating plain, poor Elsie with the girls who were usually seated beside him, he was floundering like a hooked and landed fish.

She asked how much they were asking for the horse. "I have been saving money for over two years, but I give most of my wages to my parents. Hopefully, I'll be able to afford the horse you have in mind."

"You will."

"How do you know?"

Once on the subject of the long-awaited horse, conversation came easier, although it was far from relaxed.

The summer's evening was perfect, the air heavy with maple leaves, undulating telephone wires, the manic wheeling and flocking of an assortment of small brown birds, traffic coming and going in myriad colors of blue, white, red, and black. They passed immaculately groomed lawns with colorful arrays of petunias, dahlias, marigolds. Fields full of corn growing like small trees, thick-stemmed, broad-leafed, the large, firm ears formed and yellowing. Fourth cutting alfalfa. Soybeans and pumpkin and tomato patches.

As they approached the town of Ephrata, Elam turned his horse south. Here the houses thinned some, open farmland turning to patches of woods and narrow township roads with decidedly cheaper, older dwellings. There were mobile homes and double-wides with cars parked in unmowed sections of lawn, weeds growing around them like unkempt fur.

Elsie thought it might be just a short section of these types of properties. Soon they'd emerge into an open vista of level farmland, an area where the land was cared for, well-maintained horse farms.

A German shepherd lunged on the end of a sturdy chain, barking in short, angry barks, his collar tightening. A small dog tumbled off a set of steps, flew across the yard with furious yips, his legs churning beneath him. A heavy, balding man lowered his bare feet from the porch railing and set up an awful volley of commands to both dogs, who went on with their insane howling and yelping. They traveled past that canine threat, only to find themselves surrounded by another pack of dogs of unrecognizable breed. Large brown dogs with matted coats, their ribs showing like teeth on a large comb, tails hairless with skin diseases.

Elsie couldn't help herself.

"Where are we going? These poor dogs. Surely the horse isn't here, in this . . . this area."

"Actually, he is."

He wished he'd never come, wished he had never set foot in this place. Thinking of Elsie had all been a horrible mistake.

They turned right, down a steep gravelly incline, fissured with deep, washed-out ruts, patches of weeds down the high center. The buggy tilted and lurched, threw Elsie against Elam's shoulder. The horse picked his way down as gracefully as he did everything else.

The passed a patch of woods to the right, a brown field to the left, overrun with spots of brambles and overgrown millet stalks, an old golf cart with one tire removed, holes in the roof and tufts of white insulation protruding. There was an array of rusted vehicles, like gloomy harbingers of worse times to come. A crumbling shed that had been red at one time but was brown now, with only a hint of pink between the rotting boards.

Elsie fought back despair.

What had Elam been thinking? How had he ever found this derelict place? No horse coming from this barn would be worth even a hundred dollars.

He stopped the horse, handed the reins to her, and said he'd go talk to Mr. Harris, the owner. Elsie watched him climb from the buggy and walk through the assortment of used kitchen appliances that lay half hidden in a growth of weeds. She thought this must be some cruel joke someone had thought up.

Chapter Six

TO HOLD THE REINS THAT LED TO THE MOUTH of this wonderful creature diverted her thoughts as Elam returned with an aging man, stooped at the waist, shuffling through the weeds with a pair of shoes like rowboats, laces riffling along, untied.

Without speaking, Elam led the horse to a fence, placed his hand on the post to check for sturdiness, then unhooked the rein, allowing the horse to lower his head, stretch his neck. He came back to the buggy, reached below the seat for the neck rope, tied the horse, and motioned for her to come with him.

"Elsie, this is Charlie Harris. Charlie, a friend of mine. Elsie Esh."

Elsie was sized up by a pair of rheumy eyes that still held a brilliant blue color. He wore no eyeglasses, and his nose was crisscrossed with purple veins and pockmarks like the moon's surface. A yellowed moustache hung above his puckered lips, the coarse white hair tangled and ungroomed.

"Hello, Elsie Esh. Pleased to meet you, I am." His voice was soft and whispery.

"Hello. I'm pleased to meet you, too."

"Well, good. Then we'll go see the horse."

Together they waited while the old man unhooked a two-by-four from a cast-iron brace, the only thing that held the door in place. When he swung the door back, the stench was overpowering, burning, an acidic odor of old, stale manure and fresh urine.

Elsie coughed, brought a hand to her mouth.

The light from the door was thrown unmercifully on the most pitiful sight Elsie could imagine.

"He's only four years old. A magnificent palomino. My granddaughter's. Barrel raced. Rode him at the Ohio State Fair with the Angels. He's a wonder, this horse."

The soft, breathy voice went on, explaining the loss of his granddaughter, the many events where she had shown the grand horse. Bewildered, Elsie tried to imagine this horse being ridden anywhere.

Elam stood, his thumbs hooked in his trouser belt, nodding, his eyes taking in everything.

The neck. Elsie had never seen a neck so thin on a

horse. His head was much too large, like an oversized lollipop on a stick. Coarse hair hung from his skeletal body in long, loose tufts. His thin mane hung in sections, with burrs parting the small amounts, cruel barrettes of nature.

"His name is Gold," the old man whispered.

Elsie looked at Elam, his face half averted, the light from the open barn door illuminating the pity in his eyes.

"Are you serious?" she whispered to him.

"Oh, yes. He was gorgeous."

"But he's not now."

"Do you know what can be done with a horse like this? It's why I brought you!"

He turned to face her, his eyes meeting hers squarely. She questioned. He answered with his sympathy.

Because we're poor, she thought. *You brought me here to show me this was all I could afford. That this place reminds you of ours. I have almost two thousand dollars. I can afford a nice horse.*

She swung her arm in the direction of the opened door. "You know I don't have the means to pay a veterinarian, or expensive minerals and top-of-the-line horse feed. So why think you can pawn this half-dead thing on me?"

Elsie was close to tears, and Elam was caught off guard. Misery piled on misery. It had begun badly and was ending worse. Old Charlie Harris, hard of hearing and blissfully unaware of anything amiss, kept talking in his soft breathless voice of the blue ribbons and prizes, the photographs.

When the granddaughter passed, victim of a fiery auto accident, he had taken on himself the well-meant responsibility of keeping the horse. He thought he could do it, but had fallen ill, his mental capacity deteriorating along with the aging body. The results were one broken horse who was fortunate to receive hay and water once a day, the floor of his stable rising higher with his own waste, piled in corners, turning acrid, liquid without bedding. Clots of dirt and manure stuck in his overgrown mane and tail, his beautiful legs were stained and discolored with the filth.

Elam looked at Elsie, saw the heaving chest, the passion in her green eyes, and understood. He'd had no intention of reminding her of her parents' lowly station—and what was lowly, really? Did this girl measure everything around her by the material wealth of others? Compare her own life to every situation that arose?

"Elsie."

She swung away from him, walked through the door, out of sight.

Well, nothing to do but the reasonable alternative. Turning to Charlie Harris, Elam made him an offer, which was accepted.

"Now, I know the horse needs some care. I must have forgotten to feed him a few times. Don't have the strength for the mucking out. Yes, yes. You'll do him justice. The young lady doesn't want him, then?"

"No."

"Well, that's all right. Quite all right. You'll do right by this horse. He's a winner."

Elam nodded.

The ride home was painful for them both. Quiet attempts at conversation died before they could be ignited, leaving them with a keen sense of having failed. He berated himself for the oversight. She blamed herself for having been gullible enough to be led like a blind sheep.

Before they arrived home, she had to know.

"Are you buying him?"

"Yes."

"For . . . for yourself."

"Yes."

She stepped out of the buggy before he had a chance to make amends. Never looking at him, she mumbled a goodbye and stalked into the house on legs like stilts, slapping the screen door behind her.

She went to her room and sat down hard on the edge of her bed, releasing an expulsion of pent-up frustration.

She'd always be poor Elsie, who had no taste, no smarts, not even a mind of her own. Dumber than a box of rocks. Good for nothing but winning baseball games for him. All this being "asked" was the same thing. Every young man wanted a meek and submissive wife who would hold her husband in high esteem, calling him Lord. And lordly he was, this Elam Stoltzfus. Even Benny of the smashed hat looked up to him in constant hope of being acknowledged and accepted.

Well, this drive with him had uncovered what Elam truly was, which revealed the fact that he had never changed. The same kid who wouldn't allow her to drive the Shetland pony. So arrogant. Look how he sat in that classy buggy with his wide shoulders and those solid, tanned arms covered in dark hair. She wondered what they felt like.

What? Why was she thinking about his arms? Elsie began to cry. Her face puckered and large salty tears trickled down her cheeks. She cried for every day in school when she'd eaten her cheese sandwiches facing the blackboard so no one would see. She cried for all the times she'd known the answer to difficult questions but was much too inhibited to speak up in a classroom ripe with superiority. Mostly she cried trying to figure out why Elam's arms affected her so deeply. Young men simply did not do that to her. None of them. So why now, when it was so obvious he thought of her as nothing but the poor girl down the road who could only afford a half-dead horse?

It was his nose that set her into fresh, subdued wails of wretched feelings. His nose was wide and short and blunt. It was a perfect nose set above a wide mouth with lips that were not too thin and not too full, dry, and masculine, and—oh no—really nice. She couldn't allow herself to think of his eyes that were not brown or blue or green, but the color of dried oak leaves in the fall. When an oak leaf got rained on, when it became wet, it took on a chestnut hue, a color that was not the color of anything else.

This thought brought on a fresh river of tears, until her eyes were rimmed with red and her cheeks looked like a map of the world, splotched with red and pink and purple.

She honked into a wad of toilet tissues, threw it on her nightstand, and thought of his even white teeth when he smiled. She went to the mirror above her dresser and pulled back her mouth in a grimace, her front teeth protruding like a—well, those of a horse. She broke into fresh sobs.

She sat in church with her eyes still slightly puffy, watched the long line of young men and boys file in and take their seats on the long wooden benches, Elam among them.

Determined to change everything she felt the previous day, Elsie opened her *Ausbund* with the rest of the girls and kept her face lowered as she sang, never once looking up. The fact that Elam was far too close, facing her way, made it almost impossible to raise her eyes. He must never know how much she had suffered. Was suffering.

Did he have the horse in the barn at his home? She wished she could be a hawk or an owl, to glide across the barn or perch on a window ledge, to see if the sad horse had already found a new home.

And if he was there, was he happy? Surrounded by all those high-steppers Elam's father owned, how could he be?

She knew he'd feel like her, eating her cheese sandwich, staring at the blackboard. The horse would be much more comfortable alone with Fred in their humble barn.

Horses had feelings, too. Elam wouldn't know that.

Now she was more confused than ever. If the horse was so pitiful, and she had refused to take him, how could she hope to save him except by swallowing her pride and asking Elam?

Now she had gotten herself into a gigantic, irretrievable mess, and to extricate herself meant admitting it was all her pride that had made her refuse him in the first place. She would never let Elam see this. The horse would just have to learn to be happy where he was.

She couldn't stop herself from visualizing the poor, broken-down horse, standing on three legs, the hip bones protruding like clothes racks, one leg bent, neck outstretched, that long, thin neck that just grabbed you, with the long, hard face of a much older horse, his eyes half closed in shame as the other horses kicked and stamped and whinnied, eyeing him with bold unwelcoming eyes.

Elsie tried hard to put it all behind her, to focus on the minister's face, to take in the surroundings. But everything blurred, colors running together in otherworldly chaos. When the minister spoke of kindness, she thought of the horse. When he spoke of the crossing of the Red Sea, she thought of the poor horse's inability to keep up with the throng who walked on dry land to the other side.

Then, to complicate matters even more, Elam's sister, Barbara, invited a group of girls to her house for the afternoon, Elsie among them. There she would be, not far away from the barn, unable to see for herself. If she remained quiet, perhaps Barbara would say something about the horse, and no one would ever know what had occurred.

They made soft pretzels, dipped them in cheese sauce, drank iced meadow tea, and giggled and talked before taking turns using the shower before they dressed to attend the youth gathering a few miles away.

Elsie had just stepped out of the bathroom, a white towel like a turban around her head, the cape pinned to her dark gray dress, barefoot, carrying her small piece of luggage. She felt the handle loosen and sag, looked to see if she had remembered to zip up the outside pocket, while walking hurriedly. There were more girls who needed to use the shower. That was why she plowed into a solid form, bumped the towel against it, releasing the twist on top of her head, resulting in a loose towel that slid sideways, followed by a thick, heavy ripple of gleaming wet hair.

Annoyed, she drew up short, straightened, dropped her bag, and caught herself by grasping two heavy arms covered with silky hair.

"Oh."

"Sorry."

"I . . ."

"You . . ."

She meant to let go of his arms, but she didn't.

Elam's face was very close and the hallway was in shadows. There was no one else around and everything, everything was filled with possibility. Flowers and butterflies could grow out of the walls and music could waft up from the floor.

"Elsie . . . I . . ."

"I'm sorry."

She let go, picked up her bag, and tried to push past him, but he caught her. Slowly he brought his hands up to touch both sides of her face, touch the wet hair that cascaded on either side. There were no misunderstandings, no divide of poverty or wealth, no broken horse named Gold, only two young people on the cusp of a strong attraction but kept at bay by their upbringing, by their parents' admonishing of right and wrong, and most of all, what was conventionally acceptable.

With a small cry, Elsie broke away and dashed past him and into Barbara's room, her face ashen, the wet towel lying on the hallway floor.

"What happened to you?" Florence asked.

"You're white as the walls."

Elsie laughed, a quick, breathless sound foreign to her own ears. "Guess the water was too hot. Sort of felt like passing out. Happens sometimes."

"Yeah, it can."

They went back to their hair brushing and spraying and clipping back with bobby pins and barrettes, capes pinned to a perfect V on their necklines, aprons pinned snugly around slim waists. The smell of girls' cologne stuck in the air as thin stockings were wriggled into.

Barbara walked down the hallway to the bathroom, saw the crumpled towel, found Elam lounging in the doorway of his bedroom with a slack jaw and a vacant expression, and thought, *Aha. Shower wasn't that hot. Something going on here or I'll eat this towel.*

She knew about the horse, had noticed Elam like a midwestern tornado ever since he'd taken Elsie for a ride to see him.

She'd have to help God along a bit, here. Elam had a strong admiration for Elsie now, same as he had in school. He'd told Barbara she was quite an athlete, for an Amish girl. He'd bet anything that if she wasn't Amish she'd be professional in baseball or volleyball. If she had a chance.

Which she didn't, Barbara had reminded him.

But she had forgotten all this, till now. Elam had basically lost track of Elsie over the past few years. Didn't even belong to the same group of young people.

You watch. You just watch, Barbara chortled to herself.

After the episode in the hallway, the youth gathering held no charm for Elsie. It felt like a bowl of Corn Flakes without sugar or milk. A jigsaw puzzle with no border pieces. The sun without the moon, the moon without the sun. A land without rain.

The whole atmosphere was drained of vitality. It was hard to understand, this sudden loss. If she had never known Elam, there would be no loss. But she had always known Elam. Elam and Benny. Cookie and his new horse. But that was a different time.

How could you link the two times? This Elam was like a warm campfire in a dark, cold forest. This Elam took up all your senses and threw them into the sky, where they turned to stardust, little pinpricks of dazzle in a dark sky you didn't know needed light. And having seen this transformation, you could never think of Elam as the same person driving Cookie, with Benny beside him.

She felt helpless, carried along by a deep, churning current headed straight for a high waterfall. She cried when she found a dead kitten by the side of the road. She didn't like cats, never had. But the kitten was so little and so thoroughly dead.

Her work at the bakery was like a speeding train threatening to derail. One moment her rolls were light and buttery, the sweet dough turned out to perfection. She loved her job, her coworkers. The next minute she wanted to hurl a mass of dough out a window, watch the glass split and break, tinkle to the ground in dozens of sharp sections, the dough coming to rest on top of it.

In short, everything was an unexplained mystery.

A month passed. Two.

She saw Elam in church only twice. He was never at her youth group's events, which was what she had hoped for, without admitting it even to herself. She missed something, but didn't know exactly what it was.

Sometimes she felt as if she were trying to catch white feathers that were drifting down like snowflakes, only to hurl them away the minute she touched them.

Then he showed up, knocking on the wooden frame of the screen door one evening when the cold, damp air that crept in from the northeast carried a promise of winter.

Dressed in a black peacoat and a gray stocking cap, his hands shoved in his pockets, he stepped back when Elsie opened the door.

"Hello, Elsie. How are you?"

Here he was. The border to her puzzle, the rain to her drought. The sun and the moon. But that was supposed to be God, not Elam. All this zipped through her mind as she pushed open the screen door.

"Hi. Come in, it's too damp and cold tonight."

"How are you?" he repeated.

"Fine. Good."

Now that you're here, she thought. Flustered, she tucked an imaginary *schtruvvel* from her hairline behind her ear.

Elam stepped into the bright, overheated kitchen, the woodstove at the far corner producing a steady glow. The old propane light in the cabinet by the recliner hissed steadily, throwing more heat.

He greeted the family. Her father spoke at length about the weather, saying there was to be a wintry mix till morning. He'd been hoping for a solid layer of snow for Christmas. Her mother smiled, inquired about his mother. Amos told him he was four, soon, and he was getting a trike for Christmas.

"Not the same color as my old one. Rusty-colored is my old one. My new one is red."

Elam laughed, then bent to pat his head.

"You are growing, Amos. Really growing. You better tell your mother you need a bigger tricycle."

"Trike."

"Trike," Elam agreed.

After that exchange, Elsie was weak-kneed with the understanding of what was wrong with her. It hit her like she'd been slammed into a wall.

She loved Elam more than anything or anyone else. He was her hero, her promised one, her meant-to-be.

Here he was, standing in their plain, dreary kitchen with the old appliances and torn linoleum, the scuffed chairs and faded oilcloth on the table, and everything, everything became impossible. The flowers and butterflies turned black and fell off the wall, leaving large porous holes that no amount of drywall compound or paint could fix. They were poor and crippled. The only reason he stood inside that old front door was to pity them. Maybe to offer the old horse for a few hundred dollars.

He turned to her.

"Elsie, would you like to walk over with me to see the new horse? You haven't seen him since he's been in our barn."

She stood with her pride on one shoulder, her

love on the other. She accepted without a rational thought in her head and went to comb her hair and grab a warm white scarf and her heavy coat and flew down the stairs, her eyes alight with hope.

Hope that stuffed back the impossibility, kicked away the dead flowers, but planted new seeds and would wait for the first green shoot, the first sign of activity.

They set off at a brisk pace, the night gray-black and impenetrable. Oh, lovely world. Lovely, lovely night filled with stardust and falling stars! Comets and asteroids, whole planets zipping and spinning along, filling the night sky with the wonder of all of life.

Chapter Seven

TO FIND THE HORSE LOOKING SO DIFFERENT she would not have known it was the same animal was a shock in itself, but when Elam asked her if she wanted him now, she all but fell over.

"I can't take him. Not after you've done so much for him."

"One thousand dollars," he replied.

Elsie's eyes narrowed. "How much did you pay for him?"

"Exactly that. One thousand dollars."

"Are you sure?"

He was treading on thin ice, pride and poverty and remembered school days.

"Would I lie to you?"

"Well, no. I guess not."

"So do you want him? Saddle and bridle?"

"I do. But . . . I have only ridden a horse once, maybe twice. How can I be expected to show any kind of good horsemanship? I guess, to be honest,

I'm scared. How can I compete with that old man's granddaughter?"

Elam laughed.

"You take this horse home, make friends with him, he'll do anything you say. He's sweet-tempered."

Elsie hung her arms over the side of the heavy wooden plank that made up part of the stall. She watched, took in every muscle, the rounded sides, the glassy coat, and, most astonishing, the well-proportioned head and neck. The filth and manure stains were gone, the legs were groomed to a sheer white, turning into a honey color, which spread to the horse's entire body. The mane and tail were lighter in color, as if those sections had been spun and pulled into the color of homemade taffy.

There was, however, still a droop to his eyes, as if he were still sleepy, or exhausted. The long brown lashes drooped over the deep brown eyes that seemed to glisten with tears.

"He seems tired," she said.

"Go in to him," Elam suggested.

The horse merely lifted his head and eyed her with the same tired gaze. To touch that glossy neck was like a benediction, but when he turned his head to nuzzle the front of her coat, Elsie gave in, threw her arms around the horse's neck, and hugged, tightly, laying the side of her face against his mane.

"You lovely creature. I can't believe the difference in a few months' time."

Elam stood at the gate, smiling, taking in what he had accomplished.

Elsie cleaned out the extra horse stall, swept cobwebs, washed windows, swept the old pocked concrete forebay. Malinda helped her dump the plastic half barrel that served as a watering trough and scrubbed the sides and bottom with wooden brushes and refilled it with cold, clean water. There was a rack for the saddle, a large nail for the bridle, the special feed Elam used in a fifty-pound bag that rested against the cement block wall. Minerals were in a square yellow bucket. A pickup truck delivered the best hay.

She wrote a check to Elam Stoltzfus for the wondrous sum of one thousand dollars, a check to the feed mill for $52.00, and one for $310.00

to Ronald Sanders for hay. Which meant she had spent $1,362.00, years of work at the bakery. She had a little over $800 left, which would melt away fast, buying good horse feed. Elam walked through the snow, leading the golden horse with a fairly long rope. Elsie watched them approach from the open barn door, her heart thudding against her rib cage.

What a striking figure he made. And the horse was unbelievable.

She smiled, put out a hand for the rope, and introduced Gold to Fred, who became quite animated, hopping and bouncing around in his stall like a half-grown two-year-old.

"Ach, Fred, you old geezer," Elsie laughed.

"Hey, he has a new friend. Nothing wrong with that."

Elsie saw the red ribbon braided through the mane, the bunches of greenery.

"It's lovely. How do you braid that through this coarse hair?"

"Barbara did it. I have no clue." He shrugged one shoulder. "She'll teach you."

They heard the slam of a door, and were soon surrounded by a gaggle of sisters making quite a fuss about the horse, followed by Elsie's parents and Amos.

Her father said the horse would continue to improve, that he appreciated what Elam had done for Elsie. Anyone that loved horses the way she did should have the opportunity to own one. As always, he never complained about his own lot, never referred to the loss of his arm, turning the spotlight on Elam instead of his own misfortune.

Elam lingered in the dimly lit forebay after her family had returned to the warmth of the house.

"Whenever you're ready for riding lessons, let me know, OK?"

"First I need to purchase something to wear under my dress."

"Barbara wears those stretchy things."

Elsie laughed. "Now how would I know what those stretchy things are? I'm new at this, you know. I'll probably learn to ride on my own. For a while, if you don't mind. I don't want anyone watching, knowing I'll be a genuine klutz."

"You were never a klutz at anything, Elsie."

The note of seriousness in his voice surprised her. He was not sincere. He couldn't be.

"You're making fun of me now."

"Never. I'd never do that."

"You used to."

"Not intentionally. I was always amazed at your ability in sports. I can't imagine horseback riding would be any different for you."

Elsie was speechless, flustered, and so painfully ill at ease hearing that compliment from the one she, well, she adored.

She didn't say thank you and she didn't smile or look at him. She merely shoved a sliver of wood with the toe of her boot, as if her life depended on maneuvering the small piece into exactly the right position, her eyebrows drawn down in concentration.

She heard his husky laugh, too close. She looked up, found his nearness alarming. She stepped back, grasped one hand with the palm of the other.

"Elsie, you're amazing. You'll do well," he said.

"I'll probably fall off and break my leg, or my neck. What if the horse doesn't like me?" She was babbling now. After all, she was not amazing. She was raised on coffee soup and fried mush and cheese sandwiches and never once owned a new pair of shoes and had only nine or ten dresses instead of forty. Or fifty.

She had nothing except a repainted secondhand bedroom set and a good job that paid her parents well. Well, and now she had a pretty amazing horse.

But why would Elam stand there now and act as if she were actually what he'd said?

"You don't believe me, right?"

She shook her head.

She spoke so quietly he had to bend his head to hear.

"It's hard to believe you're speaking the truth, when . . . you know, I remember what a big difference there was between us in school. And that difference has not changed."

Her words were so soft and quiet, he could barely hear, but he sensed how hard it was for her to say them.

"It's all right. We're older now. The things that mattered so much in school aren't important. It makes no difference to me if you live in a hut or a million-dollar home. It's you that fascinates me."

"Fascinates? You mean like watching a tobacco worm chew on a leaf?"

He laughed, a long, genuine sound of delight.

"Do you ever look in the mirror, Elsie? And look what happened at your job. You're a beautiful, special, talented girl, and I would love to have you for my girlfriend."

Even more quietly, Elsie whispered, "Oh, but it wouldn't work."

"What? I didn't hear you."

"Well, what I mean. Well . . . you can't want me. Not to date. Not for a girlfriend. Not seriously."

The lantern light ebbed slowly, turning the barn even darker. The light from the snow outside formed rectangles of white against the blackness of the barn walls. The wind blew loose particles of snow across the highest places, and around corners and under doors.

Elsie shivered. She was thoroughly miserable, after messing up every nice thing he had said. But the truth had to be spoken. Heartbreaks cost too much. They were the most expensive thing on earth, if pain could be counted in dollars.

She couldn't imagine her love blooming, allowing herself the freedom of loving Elam, only to have him tell her he "didn't feel right." Or he was confused, which would mean he was bored with her, was distracted, had found someone who intrigued him. So there you go, cast aside, forgotten, huddled like a beggar on the street with your heart slightly damaged forever.

Hadn't she listened to Anna Mae for hours on end? David had loved her. He had, she insisted. And then, out of thin air, his words like hatchets, he told her he didn't feel right. His feelings for her were no longer the same. Like a balloon, the air had slowly leaked out until there was nothing left but a tired, senseless little heap of nothing. Anna Mae couldn't take it. Her mother took her to see a doctor and she was put on an antidepressant to help her through the worst of it.

Elsie shook her head, the decision becoming a solid thing.

"The answer is no," she said firmly.

There was a space of silence. Old Fred snorted through his nose, rubbed his shoulder on the old wooden feedbox. Outside, the wind blew bits of snow against the barn, causing a scouring sound, as if the cold could clean the remaining slivers of paint off the drying boards.

"Can you explain the reason why?" Elam asked softly.

Elsie's thoughts scrambled, stirred together like cake batter, pride, memories, his superiority, everything, coming apart, breaking into pieces that floated around in a restless void.

She grasped at anything, one good reason that would not hurt him but would save her from exposing the smallness of her own world.

He was just too much, too wealthy, too many horses, too sought after by every girl she knew, too kind and polite and assured in his own station in life.

"I'm not good enough for you."

"Elsie, I . . ."

"No."

He left after a soft "good night." Elsie stumbled through the snow and the wind and let herself in quietly, and to bed, where she lay shivering, dry eyed.

Every girl's dream was to fall in love with a kind, talented, handsome young man like Elam, like a fairy tale, living happily ever after.

But it wasn't that easy. There were so many paths that twisted and turned, a labyrinth of feelings that always led to the same swamp of low self-worth, where she inevitably got bogged down in the mire and could see no way out.

How could he love her? He hadn't said he loved her, only that he wanted to be her boyfriend. Perhaps it was the horse, the ability to teach her how to ride, how to feed him, how to . . . well, everything. No, the match would be too uneven. Like three-fourths of a pie, her share only one fourth.

She learned to ride, through the snow and the cold.

By the time Christmas festivities began, she had already acquired the good posture, the sense of being one with her horse, who was well trained, never showing temper or disobedience.

Each day his appearance improved even more as Elsie brushed his coat, pampered and fussed with the thin mane and tail, which were showing signs of new, heavy growth. She stroked his velvety neck, under the mane, where the renewed muscle was becoming heavy and rounded. A bond of the kind that is only apparent when a human being loves an animal from the heart developed between them, and Gold responded like dry leaves to a flame. He gave his all for his new master, the girl who had replaced his first love.

The barn was the only place Elsie felt true contentment. She washed the windows with a clean rag dipped in soapy water with a dash of vinegar. She held the old porch broom to the rafters, plying it across the cement block walls and the vertical boards above it to remove cobwebs. The stalls were mucked out every day, a wheelbarrow load spread across the old barnyard, on the large garden, in the fields, anywhere there was a need for some of nature's fertilizer.

Her father grinned good-naturedly, joked that he would have gotten her a horse a long time ago if he'd known how much work she'd put into that old barn. Her mother shook her head, smiled, shrugged. They all knew that would not have been possible. But times had changed for the better. Two girls working at the bakery now meant their household income had gotten a serious raise. No longer did depleted supplies of ordinary necessities give Mam a lump in the throat, although she had always kept a brave face to her husband and all who knew her.

Christmas in the Esh household was first and foremost a celebration of the birth of Jesus Christ. Elsie and her sisters had learned at a very young age to understand the coming of the baby Jesus, the stable and the animals, the shepherds in the fields, the coming of the Wise Men to follow the star in the east. The gifts the family exchanged were simple, the Christmas dinners at the grandparents' the highlight of every holiday season. There, the cousins, aunts, and uncles brought joy, togetherness, a sense of belonging, the small gift of a book or a set of handkerchiefs a token of Daddy and Mommy's love. Elsie still had most of those books, the inside covers inscribed with the same words: "To Elsie, Christmas," followed by the year. Sometimes, there was a coloring book and a brand-new package of Crayola crayons, the yellow box still square and polished. Inside were twenty-four sharp, brand-new crayons, the greatest delight. If you colored a picture with new crayons, you could color without coming out of the heavy black lines. After the Christmas dinner, the girls spent hours coloring around the kitchen table, chattering happily, comparing colors and talents, denying the ohs and ahs of admiration from each other. They often received homemade doll clothes from their parents—little Amish dresses and black pinafore-style aprons or new flannel nightgowns for the dolls they had received years before from the thrift or consignment shops.

They exchanged names at school for trading gifts, which was a source of angst for Elsie, knowing the gift she would give would be inferior to what she received. She dreaded the opening of those packages. Sometimes she received twice, three times as much as she had given. She knew the children were all admonished to be grateful, no matter how small the gift they received from the David Esh family, so there were never any cruel remarks, only kind appreciation. But she knew.

When Elsie became older, there was the exchanging of names among the youth, but she had her own small stash of money and could buy her own gift, which meant accompanying a gaggle of shrieking girls to the expensive stores her mother never entered.

This year, Mam informed Elsie it was the first Christmas ever that she felt a sense of freedom, having the girls' market money to buy more gifts than she had ever thought possible. Her face appeared younger, unlined, uplifted, with a glow of Christmas joy. Her father's happiness was always apparent, but now he had a spring in his step, an eagerness to hitch up old Fred and accompany his wife to the Amish stores scattered along the many roads of Lancaster County. Snow drifted lazily across the countryside, already turning the brown fields to a dusting of white, like talcum powder. The macadam roads became slick, so the cars traveled slowly. They kept Fred to the right side, on the wide shoulder of the road provided for slow-moving horses and buggies, the snow spitting against the windows, settling on Fred's back, slowly melting from the body heat and sliding wetly down his sides, turning the hair on his haunches to dark streaks. It was a magical day for David and Mary Esh, gratitude filling their buggy with Christmas warmth that permeated every aspect of the joyous festivities.

For Elsie, the money she handed to her parents was no sacrifice. She had the one thing she had worked so hard to earn: her horse. The hours spent in the cold learning to ride, her face red, her eyes shining as she loped across the fields, could not compare with anything she had ever experienced. It was beyond her biggest expectations.

Now if she could only deal with this Elam Stoltzfus episode.

She told her mother about it as they coated peanut butter crackers with chocolate. Her mother stood at the opposite end of the table, her face glowing with inner happiness, a Ritz cracker spread thickly with peanut butter put together with another one on top, like a whoopee pie. She threw it into the large stainless steel bowl of melted chocolate that rested on top of boiling water, turned it with a fork, tapped the handle on the side of the bowl until the excess chocolate dropped off, then gently deposited it on the waxed paper spread on a cookie sheet.

"Oh, imagine, Elsie. Wilbur's chocolate. It's

so expensive. And I had enough, oh, more than enough to purchase it at Creekside. This is the best Christmas, ever."

"For me, too, if Elam Stoltzfus wasn't ruining it." The tapping stopped.

"Whatever!" she exclaimed, borrowing her daughter's words.

"I mean it. Mam, he said he wants me for his girlfriend. He said I'm amazing. He did. And you know it's not true."

"Elam Stoltzfus said that? Well."

The tapping continued, but a pleased smile spread across her glowing face. She placed a coated cracker carefully on the waxed paper, then faced Elsie squarely.

"And why is this not true?"

"Well, I'm not. We're . . . I am just me. None of that is true."

"I think it's true. I think he was sincere. He's been like that even when you went to school. Remember how he hung around here with that pony of his? Candy, or Cookie, whatever his name was?"

"He never let me drive."

"Elsie, you can put more peanut butter on that cracker. I have another jar in the pantry. A bigger one." She spoke with so much pride and happiness, not having to spare the peanut butter. Then she continued, earnestly. "To have someone like Elam say such a thing would not be easy. I know there is a divide in our way of living, but money has nothing to do with love. God's ways are not our ways, His thoughts far above our own piddling ability. You are an amazing daughter, talented in so many ways. In fact, everything you attempt, you excel in. Not everyone acquires their dream the way you have, through sheer hard work. You have to rise above everything that has always been our lot in life. To be poor is nothing to be ashamed of. Your father is handicapped, but rich in everything that counts. Do you realize we could be swimming in wealth, with an angry, self-absorbed father who shows no love or respect to his family?"

She picked up a tray of freshly coated crackers, a spring in her step as she carried them to the counter.

"So, what did you tell him?"

Elsie just shook her head.

Chapter Eight

THE BAKERY AT MARKET WAS CONTROLLED chaos, with Rache circling the entire area with lowered brows and a voice like a bullhorn, wedging her way between girls with clipped words of remonstration, egging them on to do more, even when it was impossible to do so.

Tray after tray of Christmas cookies was baked, arranged, wrapped, and sold. They couldn't keep the shelves filled, which resulted in harried customers lined up in frustrated rows wearing perpetual frowns of impatience. The cash register dinged endlessly as women marched off with boxes of pies, dinner rolls, loaves of bread, trays of cookies and cupcakes.

Through all the clatter around her, Elsie worked steadily, her sister Malinda at her side. Nothing distracted them from producing perfect yeast breads and rolls as they concentrated on the task at hand. It was important to allow the yeast dough to rise to the correct level, to bake the loaves just long enough in the huge commercial oven, to watch carefully that quality would not be compromised in spite of the frenzied pace around them.

It was eleven thirty, and still they hadn't had a break. Rache slammed back to the yeast dough area, flopped on a folding chair with all the force of her questionable poundage, set down two coconut doughnuts and her cup of endless cappuccino, and said she couldn't take this anymore.

"This corner is the only one that knows what they're doing. The rest is all one big hurricane. That Sheila is going to be fired unless I miss my guess. She doesn't know the meaning of the word 'hurry'. Oh, did you have your break yet?"

She bit into her coconut doughnut, closed her eyes, and moaned.

"It's almost a sin to eat something this good. Did you have your break?"

"Not yet."

"Well, go. You'll fall over, skinny as you are."

"We can't. We have to watch the proofer and the oven."

"Seriously, girls, it's not legal. You have to go. I'll watch. Go."

She stuffed the remainder of the doughnut into her mouth, pointed toward the aisles teeming with Christmas shoppers.

"Go," she said around the unbelievable amount in her mouth.

They ordered ham-and-egg sandwiches and apple juice, bent their heads in prayer, and bit into the heavenly warmth of the steaming food.

"Mm. These are the best," Elsie murmured.

Malinda nodded, her mouth full.

"I could have fainted, I was so hungry."

Elsie laughed. "Let's get another one quick. Split it. I'm never going to be full with one. I'd get an order of hash browns, but it takes that restaurant forever. We have five more minutes."

Their spirits lifted by the good food, they returned to work, not a second late.

Rache looked at the clock, shook her head.

"You girls are the best. I'll tell you. You should be paid double."

And until the Christmas rush was over, they were.

Their eyes wide, they counted their bonus, counted it again. Eli Belier thanked them both, then leaned close to ask them to keep it a secret.

"Nothing destroys a peaceful workplace faster than comparing wages. I do thank you. You continue to do an outstanding job, the biggest factor being the responsibility you take so seriously. I never worry about the yeast dough corner. Never. Don't forget our Christmas banquet the twenty-ninth, girls. Bring your boyfriend, Elsie."

She grinned, waved him away. He laughed and hurried off.

Bring your boyfriend, he'd said. Huh. If she accepted Elam, she would have that option.

On Christmas morning the girls slept in, having crept into their warm beds with limbs like soft butter, weary beyond anything they'd ever known, their Christmas bonuses tucked in a drawer. It felt almost wrong, having so much cash in an envelope.

They woke to the happy clatter from downstairs, the younger children having opened their presents early.

Elsie grabbed her robe and hurried downstairs to find Amos quite beside himself, roaring over the train set he had discovered in the large square box. Dat and Mam sat together on the couch, coffee mugs in hand, laughing, their eyes shining, allowing him to make all the outrageous sounds he wanted.

"Un train! Un train! *Gook mol*, Elsie!"

His worn flannel pajamas were red, and by the time he was finished whooping, so was his face. Elsie scooped him up, trying for a hug and a resounding kiss, but his desperate struggle to free himself prevented any affection.

The living room was warm with the crackling fire in the old black woodstove, the smell of bacon and breakfast casserole wafted from the oven, and candles glowed on the windowsill with pine boughs on the sideboard. It was Christmas.

Elsie opened her package to find fabric for a new dress, a lovely shade of green, somewhere between olive and a crayon green.

"Oh, it's really lovely, Mam. Such a different shade of green. Thank you."

"There's more," Mam said, beaming.

Elsie dug into the white tissue paper to find a small bottle of cologne, something she had never owned.

She had watched her friends spritz all kinds of floral scents liberally while she busied herself doing her hair, adjusting her covering or apron, aware of the fact that she had never been able to own something so unnecessary,

"It's too expensive," she breathed.

"Not this year," Mam said, then laughed outright, an uninhibited sound of joy and pleasure Elsie had never heard.

"The boys will notice you now," Dat said, his eyes shining over his coffee cup.

As if they hadn't already, Elsie thought, a lurch in her stomach, a stab of remembering Elam, followed by her mother's words.

Could she claim that large chunk of self-worth as her own? How did a person go about believing they were amazing? Such a thing was far too slippery, like the catfish she had tried to catch with her bare hands in the deep, dark pool in the creek. The fish looked fat and old and lazy, but the minute her hands touched the slimy scales, the fish shot away like a torpedo.

Amazing was too much. Too strong. Too hard to live up to. But Christmas cheer worked its magic and the heavy cloud of Elam and every insecurity that came with thinking of him soon vanished.

The breakfast table was boisterous, happy, with excited voices chiming into other voices until a general bedlam broke out, complete with the pinging and clacking from the battery-operated train. And then gradually they settled down to enjoy their new gifts. Anna Marie worked to complete the potholder from the new loom, plying nylon strips from one metal hook to another, her eyebrows lowered in concentration. Suvilla was wrapped in a cuddly throw, the new book from her parents held only inches from her nose.

Elsie threw on an old coat and scarf and let herself out the front door to her horse, taking deep breaths of the pristine air, the gray-white world of winter, when the sun was hidden behind a thick layer of clouds. She squinted against the white light from the snow and shivered inside the coat.

The interior of the old barn was cold, damp, but so clean. It smelled of fresh new hay, oats and corn, leather, the rusty old hydrant by the half barrel, a smell she would never tire of.

"Hey, baby."

Gold swung his head over the rough planks of his box stall, shaking it up and down a few times, as if to nod, his way of saying good morning. Elsie caught his nose, bent her head to kiss his face. She caressed his velvety ears, stroking the forelock of blond hair that hung between his eyes.

"How are you? You're a good boy. My baby," she crooned. She went to the shelf for the currycomb, opened the door to his stall, and began the daily ritual of a thorough grooming. She washed the white hair above his hooves with an old rag, then combed out the snarls in his mane and tail.

As soon as she'd be able to purchase ribbon, she'd learn how to braid his hair, the way she'd seen a horse's mane done in a magazine called *Western Horseman*. She'd been at the dentist's office and had become so lost in the world of horses and girls wearing cowboy hats that her mother had to call her twice before she looked up, the hygienist waiting patiently by the open door.

Elam would know. Not that she'd ask him, though.

She jumped, the currycomb falling from her nerveless fingers, when the door opened abruptly, letting in a rectangle of gray-white light onto the dim concrete floor of the forebay.

"Hey."

There stood Elam in the doorway of the barn.

"Oh, you surprised me."

"I bet. Didn't mean to. Sorry."

"It's ok.

"What are you up to?"

"My usual morning chores."

Elam walked past her to prop his elbows on the top plank. He whistled.

"Wow!"

Elsie smiled a very soft, hidden smile behind the hand she put up to her mouth.

"It's amazing."

"Is that your favorite word?" She was suddenly ashamed. She shouldn't have said that.

"Why, sure! It is amazing to see a transformation like this in any animal, but especially a horse. You still feeding the minerals?"

"I just ordered another bucket."

Nothing was said about the cost. Elsie appreciated his silence. It made her feel as if she were normal, ordinary, able to pay for something she needed with no questions asked.

"I haven't watched you ride him."

Elsie blushed. "You won't."

He laughed.

Then, "Do you have a ride to the Christmas singing tonight?"

Warily, she eyed him.

"No."

"Can I take you? The singing is over at Emanuel Lapp's and I'm hitching the two Belgians to Dad's bobsled. Thought we could take the field lanes, mostly dirt road. It's hard to use sleighs or sleds with the road-clearing crews at work as soon as it snows. You want to ride behind two Belgians?"

"When did you get Belgians?"

"We've always had them. These two are really showy guys, though. My dad and I bought them together. Terrible price. We'll raise colts, see how it goes."

"Why Belgians?"

"You'll see."

He knew her well enough to know she would be thrilled at the sheer size and beauty, the massive strength of these beautiful horses bred for hard work.

"Who else is going?"

"Just us. But I'm putting bales of straw and blankets in the sled so we can take spins around the fields."

She expected herself to pause, to stall and figure out how to politely answer no. Instead she said, "All right."

That afternoon, she told her parents she was going to the Christmas singing with Elam. Her mother raised one eyebrow in question from her chair, but said nothing. Her father grinned openly, in that unaffected child-like manner. But, mercifully, no one said anything.

She dressed in red, for Christmas. Her dress was a deep burgundy, a pretty shade on a fabric that draped across her shoulders with a velvety softness. She found herself humming, her cheeks flushed, as she skipped downstairs to ask her mother for help with her cape.

Malinda accompanied her back up to her room, sat on her bed with her skinny knees drawn to her chin, her eyes shining.

"Oh, I just can't wait till it's my turn to be sixteen. I simply can't wait. I'm counting the weekends. Ada and Sallie are looking forward to it as well."

"I wish you the best. I really do. It's a good time in our life, or a hard time. Whichever we choose to make it."

"You seem to be doing all right."

"I am. It's just . . ."

Elsie bit her lower lip.

"Sometimes, you're faced with hard choices."

"Like what? Guys, you mean?"

"Well, yes."

"Elam."

"Well, yes."

They laughed together, sisters enjoying the secrets and romance of *rumschpringa*.

"Elam would be my pick," said Malinda. "Except he's . . . well, you know. He's pretty sure of himself and his horses. You can see it in the way he walks and talks and drives, just everything."

"Remember Cookie?"
"Remember how mad you got?"

Elam was right on time. Bundled in her best sweater
and woolen coat, a white head scarf and heavy gloves
and boots, her covering preserved in a Tupperware
box, her purse slung across her shoulder, Elsie hurried through the twinkling light from the scattering
of stars overhead. Little dots of light decorated the
snowy landscape, and there was the smell of cold and
pine and bare branches, of decaying cornstalks.

"Hello again, Elsie," he called.

"Hello."

There were no headlights, only battery lamps
attached to each side of the massive bobsled. The
Belgians were the largest, heaviest horses Elsie had
ever seen. She had often seen them from a distance,
plodding along in some endless field, drawing a plow
or harrow, their noble heads in a powerful arc as their
leg muscles worked to do what God had designed.

Depending on what type of farm equipment they
were pulling, there were only two, hitched side by
side. Sometimes there were four, and if the plow or

the liquid manure spreader required it, there were six.

But these looked like show horses, not real farm workhorses, with all this prancing and sidestepping, as if the energy had never been directed to any menial task, certainly not drawing farm equipment.

Elam didn't say anything. He was too busy trying to hold them both to the standstill that was required until he tended to the heavy lap robes.

"Woah there, Captain. Stand still."

Elsie arranged the heavy robes herself, tucking them in beneath her legs. Laughing, she told Elam to drive, she'd be fine.

"They're quite a handful."

"I can see they are."

When he finally did loosen the reins, they lunged, but not in tandem. The left horse leaned into his collar a few seconds before the right one, which caused a jerky, uneven movement that tilted the makeshift seat, resulting in Elsie grabbing for the dashboard to keep from being thrown backward.

After that, they trotted together, their massive hooves making a dull *thlock thlock* of sound in the heavy snow, the wide bobsled runners whispering long behind them, as if the *sshhh* was meant to quiet the world around them.

The cold stung their faces. The edge of the woods appeared dark and deep, with black etchings of tree branches like crocheted lace against a lighter sky. The moon was only a sliver of cold, as if it only appeared to let the stars know who was the ruler of the skies.

Elsie shivered. She thought she had dressed warmly, but this cold, going at a fast clip against it, drove through her woolen coat and sweater, leaving her with goose bumps up her back and down her arms, her teeth clacking if she didn't press down on them.

"Cold?" Elam asked.

"No."

Not really the truth, but oh well. What could he do if she told him she was miserable?

"Want to drive?"

"We're almost at the singing. I can't."

"Why not?"

"My arms aren't strong enough."

"Sure they are. Here."

Without further words, he presented the reins to her, held them out like a proffered gift, a challenge to see if she would accept. All right. She would.

The first time her fingers closed around the heavy leather reins, she felt the magnificence. The power. It moved from those massive mouths, traveled through the steel bit and along the reins, tugged at her arms with every jingle of the harness.

It was better than riding, better than flying above the earth, better than soaring through unknown heights like a falcon. Or an eagle. It was simply indescribable, perched high on this bobsled seat, knowing the whole magical harmony of those two horses was in your control. As if for the first time in her life, Elsie felt a sense of leadership, of being the one who was able to direct these beautiful animals, in control.

She laughed out loud, a rich sound of pealing bells.

Elam watched her face and felt the despair of her resounding "No" all over again. Well, there was a reason for the old-fashioned "courting." It was the process of winning a heart. It didn't always happen immediately and he certainly wasn't about to give up that quickly.

When had she become this amazing young woman? She'd been the skinny classmate that stood at the gate in her faded, patched dresses and glared at him with those big green eyes without lifting a hand. He'd felt like a prince riding by, someone far superior to her, with that perfect Shetland pony.

The baseball in school was the beginning. She was the most graceful, coordinated girl in school, with the ability to throw a ball farther than the boys. Now she had blossomed into this beautiful girl, with so many God-given talents, he was in awe of her.

"Hold them, we're going downhill."

She nodded, concentrated on using her strength to its full advantage as the horses arched their necks, felt the slight push of the bobsled as they started down the gradual incline.

The cold winter air rushed by, numbing her face. Her fingers were stiff beneath the woolen gloves, shaking like a leaf. But she wouldn't trade the discomfort for any other sensation on earth. This was exhilarating, pure freedom.

The last stretch to the barn was level, so the horses naturally slowed their pace. Elsie put both reins in one hand, shook the other to increase circulation.

Immediately Elam offered to drive.

"No. I'll park them," Elsie said.

And she did so expertly, driving up to the circle of gray and black carriages, with dark figures unhitching horses or just standing in the cold winter night, talking, laughing together.

The bobsled slid to a halt and Elsie handed the reins to Elam. She hopped off immediately, started unhooking the traces.

"They're barely breathing faster," she observed.

"No, these guys can go all day, although at a slower pace."

"They're enormous."

"We want to do a six-horse hitch for the Ohio horse sale next year."

"Sell them?"

"Maybe. We keep buying and selling. We're always changing horses. You could come over on your days off to work with them. Learn how to braid manes, wash the fetlocks, get them in shape for shows, or whatever we need. Potential buyers or photographers are always coming around."

"You mean . . . ?"

"We'd pay you, of course. My sisters don't show much interest. They're scared of anything bigger than Cookie."

"You still have him?"

"Of course. He'll die in our barn."

"You're forgetting I'm new to the horse world. There's a lot I don't know."

"You'll learn. You can do anything you set your mind to. And you really love horses."

"I do."

"Well, then . . ."

Elsie smiled in the light of the battery lamps. Their eyes met and held. Her smile widened, and she laughed, a throaty sound of glad emotion that broke the spell. She stepped forward, clasped her gloved hands to his forearms. He felt the pressure, his heart beating so furiously he was certain she could hear.

"I'll do it."

The rest of the evening was a merry-go-round of lights and singing and faces. Colorful packages were exchanged, shouts of Christmas merriment erupted. There were Christmas cookies, meat and cheese trays, and hot chocolate. But all Elsie thought about was the huge barn filled with Belgian horses and the challenge it presented.

Chapter Nine

SHE DROVE THOSE BELGIANS THE WHOLE way home, sitting on the right, in the driver's seat, her back straight, her hands on the reins, with Elam beside her, allowing her the privilege of doing this on her own.

They did not speak, leaving the wonder of this Christmas night to engage their thoughts with the quiet tenderness of the season. Distant lights shone across the white fields, the border of trees like a dark frame surrounding a magical photograph. The stars overhead seemed to wink at them, as if they, too, knew and understood the extraordinary spirit of the night.

The whisper of the runners on snow sang the song of the ages when a young man's heart turns to thoughts of love. Elam wondered if his father heard this song, his grandfather before him, and his great-grandfather before him. How did they know who was the one they longed for? From God, that's who. The mystery of true love couldn't always be deciphered, so you just took it, appreciated it, and didn't try to make sense out of it.

For Elam, there was no one but Elsie. Plenty of girls had let him know in the way most girls do that they'd be happy to accept him whenever he felt inclined to ask them for a date. But it had never felt right, till now.

Skinny, unadorned Elsie, sitting in her desk with that old battered lunch box, ashamed of her food, her dress, her coat. And yet, when it was time to play baseball, none of it mattered. Intent on winning, her sportsmanship took over, as she turned into another person, the one who sat beside him now, concentrating on the handling of these horses that were powerful enough to run off out of control, spilling them out on the snow like corks, light and helpless.

The jingling of buckles and snaps, the flapping of leather on the horses' bodies, along with the steady, muted sound of the great hooves running across the snow filled the air. The smell of the horses' warm bodies mixed with the fresh paint of the bobsled.

Elsie's laugh broke the spell.

"The horse on the right is getting tired. He's not pulling his share," she exclaimed.

"Really? How do you know?"

"My left rein needs more pull."

He could not think of a sensible answer. If he hadn't known her his whole life, he'd have thought her a much more experienced driver.

"You can walk them."

"No, they wouldn't like that."

He opened his mouth to ask how she knew that, but closed it instead, quickly deciding he'd allow her the confidence of driving. How did she know? She was a born horsewoman. The thrill of this discovery increased his need to step back, give her time to acknowledge this talent on her own. She did not accept flowery compliments well, the ever-present lack of self-worth raising its hideous, unwanted visage.

Their arrival at her home seemed like a loss. He did not want this magical evening to be over, but was afraid to ask if he could come in for a cup of coffee. Besides, the dilapidated little barn wouldn't hold these horses, and he was positive she'd say no.

She hopped off the bobsled in one swift movement, still holding the reins, then turned to hand them over as he slid across the seat to the driver's side.

Her eyes glowed in the light of the battery lamps.

"Thank you," she said simply.

"You're welcome."

"May I thank the horses?"

"Of course."

She went around to the massive heads, stroked and murmured as they obediently lowered their noses into her gloved hands.

He strained to hear her words, but knew they were not meant for his ears.

"They're great horses. Like gigantic teddy bears. They're filled with goodness, aren't they?" she asked as she made her way back to the light from the lamps.

"I never thought about it, but yes, they are. They would never hurt anyone."

Her happy laugh rang out, like bells.

"I can't wait. When do you want me to come over?"

"You work at the bakery the last three days of the week, right?"

"Yes."

"So why don't we try for Tuesday evening?"

"Will your parents approve of having me in the barn? They won't think it's odd?"

"Why would they?"

Flustered suddenly, she tried to erase the question with a shrug.

"Oh, I don't know. Maybe your dad would think I'm too bold."

"He's not like that."

"All right. I'll be over. Good night."

The darkness swallowed her as she made her way to the house without further conversation.

Reluctantly, Elam lifted the reins, chirped to the team, and they moved off smoothly. All the Christmas cheer disappeared like the puffs of steam from the horses' nostrils.

Now why did he feel like an amateurish klutz, suddenly? *The left horse needs more pull. They wouldn't like that.* He felt the need to establish his own horse sense, make sure she'd know he was the one who would be teaching her about these huge animals. Not the other way around.

There, she'd done it again. Amazed him. In school, it was no different. He'd never seen a girl throw and catch the way she did.

He'd have to grasp his sense of superiority back as fast as he could if he meant to impress her.

Dressed in her everyday chore clothes, without adornment, the way she'd been in school, she strode up to the barn with a purposeful step, a glad light in her eye when she spied him.

"There you are!" she said, panting slightly.

"Yup. How are you?"

"Great. Excited."

"Good."

Her eyes scanned the long row of doors, the clean, wide aisle in between, the horses standing quietly behind their own partition.

"Why didn't you ride?"

"I won't ride when you . . . well, no."

"What is that supposed to mean?"

"I'd be far too self-conscious to ride when you are watching me."

"Why?"

"I don't know." She shrugged.

"Well, then we won't ride. We'll work on getting the Belgians ready for the sale in Ohio."

Her eyes shone. She clasped and unclasped her fingers. The door opened, letting in the cold white light of the winter day. His father came through the door, rubbing his hands, shivering.

"Why hello, Elsie. It's good to see you."

"Hello."

"Elam says you'll be helping out with the Belgians. Good. We're glad to have you aboard."

He noticed a strange look on his son's face and wondered.

And so began the evenings that bound them together. Elam taught her all the ways of grooming, braiding, washing and oiling fetlocks, waxing hooves, all of it a labor of love for Elsie. The best times were the hours of hitching them to various wagons, learning the proper handling of these awesome creatures.

Her favorite was the one they called Captain, or Cap for short. He seemed to take an instant liking to Elsie, responding to the slightest command spoken in her soft voice. She drove him in the high two-wheeled cart, alone, and with his partner, Caleb.

When the weather was unfit for driving, they polished harnesses, trimmed manes and tails. She proved efficient in the art of braiding colorful ribbons into the heavy manes as well as grooming the bodies of the great beasts until they shone with a deep copper glow.

Elsie and Elam talked as they worked, about everything and anything. She learned many things about him, including the insecurities he harbored about being what his father expected of him, which came as a surprise.

"I didn't think you knew what it felt like, trying to live up to someone else's standards," Elsie remarked, stopping midstroke to stare at him, her arms hanging loosely at her sides, the currycomb in her right hand.

"You don't know my father. He's a very precise person. When you think you've managed to come up to his standards, he raises the bar."

She noticed the flicker of self-doubt in his dark eyes, the slight twitch of the corners of his mouth, as if he were remembering a past episode that brought unwanted emotion. His face was becoming a familiar map, one she scanned so often she was coming to know every contour, every flash of his eyes, or the softening of them. She knew by the sound of his voice when he was frustrated and when he was pleased. She knew when the pressure was on, like today, that he would always bring up the subject of his father.

"We're driving four at the horse sale. Four. Cap, Caleb, Doll, and Dominic. I want you to do it. He says I have to, but I know you're better. He won't accept it."

Elsie's mouth hung open in disbelief, her eyes wide as she gazed at him.

"You think I can?" she whispered.

"You've done it."

"Two. Never four."

"Today, we'll do it. I'll show him."

His mouth was set in a determined line.

The February weather accommodated the hitching up, the sun warm on their backs, a brisk wind in their faces. The horses were full of energy, prancing, sidestepping, lowering their noses to the piles of gray-white snow scattered across the wide area in front of the barn. Elsie's skirt was tugged first one way then another, her headscarf threatening to leave her head. They worked together, calming the horses, fastening traces, checking and rechecking the harnesses, every buckle and snap.

Elam told her the horses had to learn obedience perfectly, so they made them stand still, in spite of the wind and their own high energy. It was a thrill to be able to master these powerful animals' will, to know that a spoken word would enable both of them to stand back, admire the clean silhouette of this amazing hitch.

At the last minute, Elam's father came out of the house, buttoning his coat, his walk purposeful, as if he regretted having allowed this without his supervision.

"You didn't tell me you were hitching four," was his greeting.

"I think I told you this morning," Elam replied.

He looked over the team with a trained eye.

Elsie watched Elam's face for any sign of fear, but there was none.

"I thought Doll worked best behind Dominic," his father said.

"Behind? They're a team," Elam answered.

"As long as you know what you're doing."

With that, he strode off, leaving Elam with a flicker of doubt, a waning confidence. He turned to Elsie. "You drive."

For only a second, she sensed the little boy's disappointment in him. He had not quite come up to his father's expectation. Did he ever?

To see this in the one who always showed absolute confidence, perceived as arrogance more than once, was astounding.

So he was not as sure of himself as he would have the world believe.

She took a deep breath and looked at the four massive horses, their flanks quivering with the cold and the eagerness to run. This wagon was no bobsled. It was twice as high and glossy, the wheels like wet pine wood, the color of caramel. The body of the wagon was painted a deep burgundy, with the same caramel color repeated on the seat. The first time she'd seen the wagon, she'd gasped in disbelief.

She had never imagined anything like it, didn't know such beauty existed in the form of a horse-drawn wagon. It was borrowed from Bailing Springs Stables for the show.

She shook her head. "I don't know about this."

"You won't until you try."

He handed the reins to her. She scrambled up the wide iron steps. He stayed at Captain's head, watching intently as she took a deep, steadying breath.

"You OK?"

She nodded.

He came around to the other side and was up beside her.

"Gloves?"

She nodded.

She had never been so afraid in all her life. This was different than driving two, and that in itself inspired awe.

When she loosened the wide leather reins and called the command to start, her voice was high. Her breath came in quick gasps.

She did not feel the cold, or the warmth of the sun. Everything faded away, leaving only the backs of the horses, the black symmetry of harness, buckles, rings, and polished adornment.

She concentrated on the four arched heads and necks with the intricacy of the woven manes, the red ribbon intertwined with the oatmeal-colored manes. Sixteen massive hooves crunched on gravel, the huge wheels moving effortlessly. They had moved off together in a perfect rhythm, which was amazing. But she knew they'd spent hours being trained for this.

The road loomed like an insurmountable hurdle. Could she make the turn?

Elam didn't speak. He gave her no instruction, merely sat watching for traffic as if this were an occurrence that happened every day for both of them.

All right.

She remembered the softness of a horse's mouth. She eased into the drawing of the reins, her hands light, but feeling the power and obedience.

"Car," Elam said softly.

Her first impulse was to haul back on the black reins with all her strength, but she pulled lightly, concentrated on distance, the ability to stop before the car's approach.

She waited, the car went past, and she loosened the reins, drawing slightly on the right. She couldn't make a tight turn, so she allowed a slight maneuver.

The horses responded as one.

The turn was executed flawlessly.

"Perfect!"

Elam was grinning, watching Elsie, who never took her eyes from the team, her back straight, her hands held at the proper angle, her profile showing pure concentration.

"Great. You're doing great."

She said nothing, allowed no smile of recognition.

Traffic almost stopped. The occupants of passing vehicles gawked like schoolchildren. Cell phones were held out of windows as their picture was taken repeatedly. Cars pulled to the side of the road, motorists scrambling to record the massive four-horse hitch on their phones to show the world.

Elsie was not distracted. She kept her eyes on the horses, her hands steady on the reins as they moved along the country roads of Lancaster County, making a huge circle before coming from the opposite direction, slowing to make the turn into the Stoltzfus driveway.

They drove up to the barn, where the dark figure of Elam's father emerged immediately, a scowl on his weathered face, his hat pulled low.

"Why'd you let her drive?" was his way of greeting.

"She'll drive at the sale."

"Not without my permission."

There was nothing to say to that, so they climbed down, one on each side, beginning to loosen traces as they averted their eyes. He watched, without comment, then turned away and left.

Benny came flying out of the house, his coat flapping behind him as he struggled to shove his arms into the sleeves. He had long since abandoned the torn straw hat, but his long bangs took the place of having to peer at his surroundings through the brim of his hat.

"Hey, you guys!" he shouted. "Why'd you leave without me? Huh? Sneaking off so I don't get to ride. I bet you got your picture taken? Huh? I could have been on there."

"Too bad," Elam called, grinning at his younger brother.

"Can I drive next time?"

"Probably not."

"Is that right? I'll ask Dat."

"Look, Benny, you don't have an interest in these horses. There's a lot more to it than having your picture taken. You're never with us, you have no idea how to drive, or hitch them up or anything."

Benny changed the subject. "I'm going for pizza. Wanna come with me? Me and Rueben."

Elam lifted his eyebrows to Elsie.

The truth was, she was starved. She'd been too nervous to think about eating all day. But with Benny and his sidekick? She nodded.

After the horses were rubbed down, stabled, and fed, and the wagon shoved into the garage, they cleaned up in the house. Elsie was shy and quiet, borrowing a clean apron from his sister. She tried not to gawk at the immensity and beauty of the house. Elam and she were still worlds apart.

"You have to get in the back," Benny informed them, after he led his horse and buggy up to the yard.

Elsie stiffened.

She wasn't aware of any young man having a back seat available. Normally, the youth crowded in the front, the back full of all the paraphernalia young *rumschpring* carried with them.

"Why do you have Dat's carriage?" Elam asked.

"My brakes are shot. Came down Welsh Mountain and burned them out over the weekend."

There was nothing to do but climb into the back and submit to the intimacy of the back seat of a buggy, which is a small space, at best, knees shoved up against the front seat.

Benny was a terrible driver, talking nonstop, lurching to a grinding halt, then chirping and shaking the reins over the unsuspecting horse's back, causing the buggy to be yanked forward. He drove off the road repeatedly, resulting in a clunk as the right wheels dropped off the macadam, onto the gravel shoulder, throwing Elsie against Elam, who took full advantage of the closeness, wrapping an arm protectively about her shoulders.

Rueben was picked up and the two started in with their constant jokes. Elsie laughed so hard, tears ran from her eyes as she bent forward, which enabled Elam's arm to tighten even more.

The pizza was delicious, the dim light another

intimacy with Elam painfully handsome beside her. Everything seemed surreal, the giddiness of having driven the four-horse hitch successfully, the joy of looking forward to the sale in Ohio, knowing she would soon ride Gold with Elam on his riding horse, as all her insecurities and inhibitions melted away in his company.

And later, she blushed to think that, yes, when that arm came around her shoulders on the way home, she had leaned in slightly—maybe more than slightly.

Oh, the feeling of being wanted and protected, though. She had never imagined the quiet assurance of growing into something she labeled "like." She liked Elam. Love, the heart-throbbing captivity of falling in love, was too much. This kind of friendship was perfect.

Chapter Ten

FOR ALL THAT YEAR, THEIR FRIENDSHIP DEEP-
ened. They fed horses, braided manes, cleaned stalls.
They stood in box stalls ripe with the smell of fresh
horse manure, leaned on pitchforks as they talked.
Sometimes they argued, when Elsie could not control
her tongue, when she felt passionately against one of
Elam's decisions.

They rode together, sometimes holding hands, the
creak of leather, boots in stirrups, the nodding of the
horses' heads, the ring of an iron-shod hoof on rock.

And still they did not date officially. He never
asked her out on a real date, so no one knew about
the developing relationship.

Elam's father watched with a wary eye, but never
said a word. His mother knew, but figured it was best
to stay quiet. That girl had more horse sense than
anyone she'd ever known, and if horses were what
it would take to get those two together, then so be
it. Elsie was who she wanted for Elam. Unspoiled,

taught in all the ways of submission and obedience, she would be the perfect match for Elam's strong will and spontaneity.

Sometimes they spent a weekend together, but always with a group, never giving away the friendship that had developed already. She drove the four-horse hitch at many events, Elam beside her, her gloved hands soft but firm and capable. She looked forward to each event, but concentrated on extra training beforehand, doing the work, inspecting harnesses, braiding and rebraiding manes until they passed her expectations.

She grew to love the crowds, the yells, the hat throwing, the thunderous cheers. Her confidence increased every time they made successful drives around the ring, which pleased Elam. She had even taken to standing up to his father. There was never anything done quite right, always a buckle too loose, a strap too tight, a braid not bound tightly enough. Small, irritating things she had hurried to correct, before. When the horses were loaded into the comfortable trailer, tethered, and given sufficient attention, he stood by the gate as they raised it, stern and imposing, as always.

"You should have loaded Dominic first."

"Why is that?" Elam asked, clapping his hands to rid them of dust, then bending to brush off his clean black trousers.

Elsie stood waiting.

"He's the most aggressive."

"And why would it make a difference when he was loaded?"

His father's eyes met those of his son, the thread of dislike decipherable by the pronounced scowl on the elder Stoltzfus, and the downward twitch, the vulnerable arc of the sides of Elam's mouth that always tore at her heart.

Elsie stepped forward, her arms crossed loosely across her waist.

"Dominic does best on the right, at the very front, on account of the traffic. That's why he's loaded there."

She could see the arrival of his taunt, his dismissal of her judgment, could see the correcting of it, the instant smile of condescension.

"Ah yes, Elsie. You're learning fast."

"I am. And I do appreciate that you allow me to work with the horses. It's a lifelong dream."

"Just make sure you take 283, and not 30," he said gruffly, and strode off.

Elam muttered something about him not being the driver. The driver had his wife along, which meant they would share the second seat of the dual-wheeled pickup truck with the immense trailer attached to it. They talked the whole way, conversing in Pennsylvania Dutch, mostly about the relationship with his father.

"I mean, come on. Why would we take 30, with four horses? That route is OK if you're not in a hurry, but what was he thinking? He always manages to make me feel like I'm ten years old."

"I think it's most fathers and their oldest sons. I really do. It's normal. He knows you're better with the horses than he is. He knows we've taken these horses to a level he never thought possible."

"You're right."

"So don't worry about it. He needs to feel as if he has accomplished all this, not us. It's a man thing. I can tell he hurts you with his words, but let him have that sense of authority by picking on little things. It makes him feel important."

"He needs to grow up."

"So do you."

"Harsh words."

"Necessary words."

Their eyes met and held. They both smiled. It was a smile that made Elsie feel wanted, respected, accepted, elevated to a position of absolute trust. They knew each other so well, could openly discuss every situation, every slight feeling of annoyance or anger, every joy, every accomplishment.

And yet, it never dawned on them that they probably should be dating in the conventional way. Perhaps if they did, all this would be lost, this shared intimacy of building a perfect four-horse hitch. They made the wide curve from Route 283 to the Pennsylvania Turnpike entrance, slowed while the driver positioned the EZ pass scanner, then resumed their speed as they traveled west.

"Another few hours and we'll be there. Altoona isn't more than a hundred miles, maybe a hundred twenty."

Elsie sat back and enjoyed the view of the wide Susquehanna River, the towering apartment and office buildings in Harrisburg.

Three Mile Island was steadily spewing the steam from the nuclear plant, with other, smaller islands dotting the river like moles on a face. Elsie loved the river and wished she could camp on that largest island; she pointed it out to Elam.

"I'll take you camping sometime. But not here, on these islands. You wouldn't be allowed."

"Seriously?"

For Elsie believed everything Elam said. He was the wise one, the knowledgeable one. But when it came to the horses, she was his equal. And finally, she knew it.

Her work at the bakery was no longer a challenge. All she really cared about was Elam and the horses, and not necessarily in that order. To be able to groom them, braid the manes, and oil the fetlocks was nothing like the repetitive motion of doing hundreds of yeast rolls and bread, cinnamon rolls like an expanse of sweet dough she automatically peppered with cinnamon and brown sugar, her hands flying effortlessly while she talked to her sister Malinda.

Rache, the eagle eye of the entire business,

confronted her before the Christmas rush. In her normal abrasive manner, the ever-present tall cup of cappuccino clutched in her sausage fingers, she stood without speaking, a huge and intimidating presence.

"So, what are your thoughts about your job?"

Confused, Elsie stopped rolling the length of dough. She turned to look at Rache, one eyebrow arched in question.

"What do you mean, my thoughts about my job?"

"Well, you're awfully preoccupied. Your thoughts aren't on your work. I asked for two batches of iced raisin bread, and what did I get? Only one."

Elsie blushed, stammered.

"Surely not."

"Yeah, it's true. Now there are only two loaves on the shelf."

"I'm sorry."

"Sorry isn't going to correct the problem."

"I'll do another batch."

"You can't. You have all you can do with the iced cinnamon rolls. I don't know what Eli will say."

Elsie felt the heat rise within her. The old Elsie would have quivered in her shoes, frantically apologized, afraid she'd lose her job, at worst. But now, she felt a new confidence. The same backbone she felt as she climbed effortlessly onto the high wagon seat and took the reins in her hands, looked out on the beautiful symmetry of those four wide backs and the colorful, intricate weaving of the manes, and knew those magnificent creatures trusted her as she trusted them. She held the power to make them obey with the reins in her hands, knew when one horse was nervous, jumpy, and knew what to do about it.

Now, she knew Rache was used to the power of the upper hand, knew she could display all kinds of authority, being Eli's right hand, and reveled in it.

Elsie knew, too, that one batch of raisin bread was not a big deal. Not even close to what Rache was hoping to make it.

"I'll do it. No problem."

"It is a problem."

Malinda worked furiously, her back turned, her head lowered in submission.

Elsie drew herself up to her full height, her hands on her hips, and looked at Rache squarely. Her eyes were like wet raisins in mounds of dough, shining with grease.

"As soon as you remove yourself from this space, I can get to work on it. If you need to tell Eli, go right ahead. For all the years I have worked here, he has never complained about my work, and I'm sure I have made more mistakes than one batch of raisin bread."

Elsie lowered her hands and made shooing motions, to get her to remove herself.

"Go. I need to get started."

"Growing up, are we?" was her parting shot, but she moved off, like a great lumbering ox, holding the cup of cappuccino like a sword.

"Elsie!" Malinda hissed.

"Sorry, Malinda. But it's time she knows I am no longer afraid of her."

The bakery fairly sizzled with activity as Christmas approached, and Elsie did her best, the way she always had.

Somehow, she knew the old ways to please Eli and to astound Rache with her abilities were faltering. Like a gasoline engine that was running out of fuel.

Her heart simply was no longer in the work at the bakery.

Yes, she needed the money. Her feed bill came regularly every month, and her parents depended on the extra amount, now doubled by Malinda's pay. Her mother had confided in her about being able to "put away" a rather large sum for her cedar chest made at Dannie King's woodworking shop. She would buy towels and sheet sets in January, when some of the local dry goods stores held their sales.

"Maybe even Walmart." She spoke reverently, with a hidden delight at being able to do as other mothers did, to fill the hope chest with linens, tablecloths, and kitchen towels, the marriage of a daughter like northern lights in a dark sky.

She was in awe of her daughter Elsie. But still, lovely though she was, it was necessary to stay humble. She could be dating now. She'd heard from her sister that a half dozen boys, if not more, had asked her.

She turned them all down, crazy to be with those Belgians on the Stoltzfus farm. Or was it the son?

Well, she'd go ahead and get that hope chest filled up, a luxury she could not have dreamed of before the wonderful high-paying job at the bakery.

God would provide, she'd always said. And now He had.

Elsie knew she did not want to live the remainder of her years providing for her family. She longed for a home of her own.

To be able to get up in the morning and make breakfast for someone she loved, to do laundry, clean her own house, work in her own garden, the added bonus of being able to work with the horses. . . .

What? Where had that thought come bubbling out of? To daydream about her own home had nothing to do with the Belgians, or Elam. Did they? Did it?

Oh, but it did. Elam and the Belgians and Gold, Cookie, old and graying around his nose, all of it, everyone was included in her hopes for the future. It was all she wanted.

And yet, he had never popped the question: "Elsie, may I take you home? Elsie, may I ask you for a date?

May I pick you up on Saturday evening? Around seven?" Since that night she turned him down so long ago now, he hadn't once broached the topic.

As time went on, she came to believe their friendship was merely that, a friendship and perhaps a professional partnership.

The weekend in October when they trucked the riding horses to Mount Gretna to go trail riding in the mountain with the colorful foliage was a bit of heaven on earth. They'd talked of their relationship, how well they got along, how one knew what to expect of the other, even laughed about it. The look in his eyes contained an ownership, a pride in her, so that her heart quickened. She was so sure he would turn the conversation to serious plans of beginning a formal courtship.

Sometimes, he held her hand when they rode, their knees touching as the horses walked in rhythm, the creak of stirrups and saddles whispering their close feelings.

On the trail ride, he told her she was beautiful.

That was all, though, which was much like drinking unsweetened tea—it was good, but she had hoped for more.

And here was the Christmas season again, a time of joy in the savior's birth, the giving of gifts to one another to follow the tradition of the wise men, and she was left with the impending wisdom that she'd have nothing from Elam but a tall glass of unsweetened tea. And another and another.

There were no horse shows or sales till January. The Belgians were in top-notch condition, so Elsie stayed home in the evening, pampered Gold, took her brother, Amos, for rides, sitting astride like a mighty little warrior as the cold wind scoured the brown fields, sending bits of corn fodder aloft, whirling madly in any direction.

Amos loved the golden horse, spent all his time at the barn with Elsie, jabbering away in his lisping voice.

He told her that if he ever got married, he and his wife would have a llama farm with horses to chase them around and a red Farmall tractor to haul the dead ones away.

Elsie threw back her head and laughed.

"You funny boy! Now why would your llamas die?"

"A fox would get them."

Elsie laughed again, a deeper, richer sound.

And then he was there, his dark form filling the lantern light, a wide grin on his face. Elsie saw him and stopped laughing.

Amos said sternly, "Elam's here."

"I see."

It was all Elsie could think of. He appeared different, somehow. His face was pale, drawn, as if he were not feeling well. His eyes were serious, dark, as if he had experienced a sobering event that he needed to share with her.

"I had a ride on Elsie's horse," Amos told him. "We just got back. We're cleaning up the forebay. Where's your horse?" Amos asked, his face like a cherub peering out from the lowered stocking cap.

"I didn't bring my horse. I walked."

"Not even Cookie?"

"I wouldn't fit on Cookie too well these days," Elam replied. And still he did not smile.

He said, "Can I talk to you, Elsie?"

She gestured toward Amos, raised her eyebrows.

Elam nodded toward the house.

"Bedtime, Amos. I'll take you to the house."

"Why?"

"It's late."

When she returned, Elam was finishing the job of sweeping wisps of hay. He looked up, his face still a set mask, like a wax figurine.

"That didn't sit well with him," she said, hoping to lighten his mood. "He wanted to tell you about his llama farm."

Elam merely lowered himself onto the old express wagon, as if his knees would give way if he stayed on his feet a minute longer.

"Sit down, Elsie."

He patted the seat beside him. She bent to scrape away the wood chips and bits of bark left on the wagon from hauling wood from the shed into the house.

"What's wrong, Elam? You don't have the flu that's going around, do you?"

"No, I . . . I'm all right."

A silence hung between them like a veil, the only sound the steady grinding of Gold's teeth as he chewed the good hay.

The battery lantern shone steadily, its white light illuminating the shabbiness of the old barn, the cracked windowpanes, the one replaced by a piece of plywood, the blue plastic half barrel set on cement blocks for a watering trough.

She felt the old misery of being poor, of having this half barn, half shed as a shelter for the beautiful Gold. And Fred. Fred, the old, plain Standardbred driving horse with his discolored halter, torn on one side.

Well, this was who she was. Plain Elsie. Davey Esha ihr Elsie. Handicapped Davey, with one hand and most of his arm missing. And they were doing well. They had remained independent, had made a living, even if it had always been a bit hardscrabble. They had risen together as a family, buoyed by love and kindness, tremendous caring for each other, and Elam would simply have to look for another girl if she would never be good enough.

"Elsie. I miss you."

"Well, I'd be over, but it will be another few weeks till Christmas is past. We're really busy at the bakery."

"No. I miss you more than I can say."

"But . . . I don't . . ."

"I can't go on another day without telling you how I feel about you. I'm not good with words, OK?"

She nodded, dumbfounded.

"Do you ever think of me in the way that . . . I mean, do you come over to help with the horses for just that? The horses? Or do I count?"

"Well, I . . ."

Why aren't you dating? Most of your friends are."

"I just never wanted to."

"You still don't?"

For a moment that seemed like hours, Elsie did not give him an answer. Who was she to tell him? He would not understand.

"I guess not really, or I would have accepted."

"Accepted who?"

"You know. The ones that have asked me out on a date."

"Yeah. I guess. Why didn't you take them?"

"I don't know."

This was going all wrong. Elam had the distinct sensation of being bogged down in unrelenting mud, with no available help.

Elsie wanted to tell him she wasn't dating because she could not accept anyone except him. His beloved face was the one she wanted to see when she woke up in the morning, the face that would be across the table from her at every mealtime. He was her friend, her confidant, the one who knew everything about her, every dream, every goal, her attitudes both good and bad.

"So you won't be dating anytime soon?"

Elsie took a deep breath to steady herself, embracing the clear and precise feeling of flinging herself off a cliff, abandoning all convention and common sense.

"I can't date anyone when it's you I love," she whispered.

She felt him draw back, heard his sharp intake of breath.

"What did you just say?" he asked hoarsely.

"I love you, Elam. No one else."

"Elsie," he said thickly.

He stood then, and reached for her hands. He drew her up, his eyes never leaving her face. He dropped her hands, his going to her face.

"Beautiful, talented girl. I can't believe what you just said. Elsie, you are the love of my life. A love that grew so big it was way out of proportion, and became scary and, well . . . I'm not much of a man, I guess. After that first time when you turned me down, I never had the nerve to tell you how I felt."

And then he drew her close, found her lips, and kissed her with a great tenderness, a quiet longing. Elsie was carried away to the place of a love that was real, a hundred times more than she could have imagined.

The old barn with the leak in the roof became a haven for the two people who felt the beginning of a love that would last a lifetime. The kind God gives freely to those who love Him, the enduring love that rides on the wings of admiration and respect.

Outside, the first snowflake of the season settled on the rusted old roof and winked at the two of them as it slowly melted into a tiny rivulet of winter. Christmas bells rang deep and true across the land, some evening service coming to a close as the silvery snowflakes came down in earnest, blessing the two as they remained in each other's arms, a declaration of the wonder of love.

Glossary

Alaubt—allowed
Ausbund—songbook
Gook mol—look
Kopp-duch—head scarf
Maud—maid
Roasht—roast chicken and filling
Rumschpringa—a time of courtship, in which Amish
    teenagers participate in organized social events
Schtruvvel—disheveled
Schtruvvlich—messed-up hair
Ungehorsam—disobedient

OTHER BOOKS BY LINDA BYLER

LIZZIE SEARCHES FOR LOVE SERIES

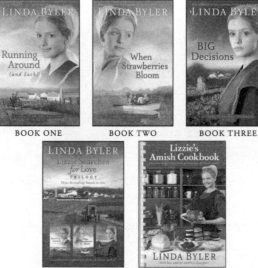

BOOK ONE   BOOK TWO   BOOK THREE

TRILOGY   COOKBOOK

SADIE'S MONTANA SERIES

BOOK ONE   BOOK TWO   BOOK THREE   TRILOGY

LANCASTER BURNING SERIES

| BOOK ONE | BOOK TWO | BOOK THREE | TRILOGY |

HESTER'S HUNT FOR HOME SERIES

| BOOK ONE | BOOK TWO | BOOK THREE | TRILOGY |

THE DAKOTA SERIES

| BOOK ONE | BOOK TWO | BOOK THREE |

| THE LITTLE AMISH MATCHMAKER | THE CHRISTMAS VISITOR | MARY'S CHRISTMAS GOODBYE | BECKY MEETS HER MATCH | A DOG FOR CHRISTMAS |

About the Author

LINDA BYLER WAS RAISED IN AN AMISH family and is an active member of the Amish church today. Growing up, Linda loved to read and write. In fact, she still does. Linda is well known within the Amish community as a columnist for a weekly Amish newspaper. She writes all her novels by hand in notebooks.

Linda is the author of six series of novels, all set among the Amish communities of North America: Lizzie Searches for Love, Sadie's Montana, Lancaster Burning, Hester's Hunt for Home, The Dakota Series, and the Buggy Spoke Series for younger readers. Linda has also written five Christmas romances set among the Amish: *Mary's Christmas Goodbye*, *The Christmas Visitor*, *The Little Amish Matchmaker*, *Becky Meets Her Match*, and *A Dog for Christmas*. Linda has coauthored *Lizzie's Amish Cookbook: Favorite Recipes from Three Generations of Amish Cooks!*